THE CHOICE

LOVINE

HAROLD

The

MYRA

Choice

illustrated by
Jos. E. DeVelasco

TYNDALE HOUSE PUBLISHERS, Inc. Wheaton, Illinois

First printing, paper, September 1981

Library of Congress Catalog Card Number 80-52236, cloth
Library of Congress Catalog Card Number 81-52207, paper
ISBN 0-8423-0249-2, cloth; ISBN 0-8423-0248-4, paper

For
HAROLD FICKETT
and
PHILIP YANCEY
who kept pressing
for ever more creativity
and clarity

CHAPTER ONE

SHE awakened, opened her eyes and saw, in her first light, Aaael's face lifting her to life. She rose from the earth, her eyes upon his, drawing her first breath from him.

She inhaled fragrances: quince blossoms, marjoram, lime-flowers, cedar. She moved her eyes and saw, indistinct against the sunlight, the membranes of aspen leaves. Music from birds and animals, from heavenly spheres and celestial beings, reverberated into her awareness as all creation began to celebrate.

She saw a gazelle staring at her, a falcon in flight, rapids in the river, a bush thick with red peonies. But the joy flowed from Aaael, and her dark eyes kept returning to his face.

She looked down at her body. She rotated her left foot, then fluttered her fingers, bent her knees. Intrigued by her long, black hair, she rubbed it against her skin, then divided it into smaller strands, contrasting them with her fingers.

The songs of the watching universe were lifting her like the rhythmic beating of wings. She sang, then, and suddenly realized that Aaael, too, was singing of his own delight in his new creation.

Aaael's thoughts flowed with his music through her and she sensed he was leading her to a form which lay upon its side in the grass. It was a man, his head resting on his forearm. At Aaael's touch he moved his shoulder, then stretched his legs downward. He rose to his feet slowly, as from a deep sleep. When the man noticed the woman, he started forward and stared. She was puzzled at seeing him, wondering if he were an image of her own body.

The man moved toward her. She reached out, touched his beard, then her own soft cheek. All life, all emotions, were new to the woman. Yet it was only the man who made her tremble so pleasantly. "You are like me, but not me," she said to him.

"You can speak!" the man said. "In every way, you're flesh of my flesh!"

The man and the woman conversed then, the man sharing his knowledge with her.

"Your name will be Risha," he said, "for you were taken from me."

"And you?"

"I am Kael."

THE woman walked lightly, still quivering with wonder. She studied every convergence of color, every sparkle from the sun, every scent and texture. Risha touched a ridge of bark, lifted an iris to inspect its fragile veins, rolled a smooth stone in her palm. She emerged from the forest on a rock ledge above the river, and the sensation of a blossom against her neck stopped her. *A pleasant feeling,* she thought. She touched the purple flower, soft like a pansy, but as wide as her arm outstretched. With her fingertips she explored the streaks of yellow sharply contrasting with purple. The texture of both colors was identical. This puzzled her, and she rubbed her fingertips back and forth over them.

Risha touched the huge blossom against her cheek. The slight tickling made her smile. She threw her arms around the flower, letting the ragged edges titillate her skin. Suddenly the blossom broke from the

8

stem and tumbled into her arms. She laughed aloud and pulled several more blossoms to her, until, her arms held low before her like a basket, they covered most of her body.

She heard footsteps behind her and tried to imagine the impact of Kael's flesh against dirt. She pushed her own foot against the ledge, then stamped it lightly to hear the sound.

Whisperings of Aaael moved in her mind, prompting her to leap unafraid from the ledge. She plummeted toward the water below as the purple and yellow blossoms floated in the breezes above her.

Hitting the water startled her, but she felt no pain, only the pleasant sting against her firm new muscles and then the water above her. As she broke the surface, she heard Kael's body hit the water and his head soon appeared beside hers. "You astonish me, Risha!"

"Do I? Everything in your world astonishes me!" She laughed, but the movement bobbed her down and she had to kick her way to the surface. Water had entered her mouth, and she now tasted it, swished it over her tongue and teeth, swallowed it and tasted again, considering it very good. "It was Aaael who said I could leap off like that," Risha said.

"Have you been with him on other worlds," Kael asked, "that you talk with him so much?"

"Other worlds?" She kept treading water and looked around her. "I don't know of any world but this. Look!" she demanded. "What's that splashing among the blossoms?" The petals had broken up and the sun glints looked like golden pollen among them.

"Fish," Kael explained. He lunged at one of the splashes and grabbed a little pipefish, gold with streaks of red. He tossed it to her but she missed so that it fell back into the water.

"Strange little creatures," she observed as they nipped at the flowers. She swam under the water, studying their fins and tails from below. Risha could see the fish as clearly as if they were swimming in air: tall dorsal fins of brilliant red above bright, almost glowing emerald backs; transparent fish with white bones and lace-like tails. She saw ribbon fish a foot high and twenty feet long with streaks and diamonds; mantas with checkered patterns of yellows and greens; black swordtails with bold apricot and vermillion markings; silver-white sticklebacks with pale blue eyes; polychromatic eels.

As they swam, they turned a bend in the river and in a small cove she saw above her—rushing, it seemed, out of the sky itself—water, cascading down and creating a fountain of bubbles. She swam toward the waterfall, then felt her knees and hands touching the pebbly bottom. As she rose and tried to step into the waterfall, the turbulence flipped her back. She grinned and tried again, but was again flipped backwards. She lay prostrate and crawled into it, but it struck her head and shoulders and pushed her quickly into the shallows.

They continued to romp at the waterfall, then turned to swim around the inlet. The fish sped between Risha's legs as she kicked, leaped over her head as she drew breath, and darted directly toward her, then dropped away at the last moment just under her plunging arm and hand.

They reached shore together, but Risha kept peering into the water to locate yet another ghost shrimp and watch it rush backwards.

"Come up the hill," Kael invited.

She suddenly felt Kael's emotions penetrating her own. Startled, she reached for Kael's arm and pulled him toward her. She could see in his face the same anticipation invading her. It was Risha's first experience with her *empath* sense. "Kael," she said to him, "I can *feel* how pleased you are with what you're going to show me."

"Yes," he agreed, then said without a trace of self-consciousness, "This is my work." He led her to a hill where his meticulous grafting had produced giant blossoms which decorated the bases of willows, banyans, and macadamias.

DEVELASCO © 80

A few yards before her, very tall, thin, leafless trees rose bone white to the sky in a large circle. Green, lacy plants like seeding asparagus rose to the same height and seemed to dance among the white branches. At their trunks were bushes, crimson red except for flecks of ochre. These seemed to race like flames through and around the circle. Black stones edged the circle and then formed a fish shape beyond it, pointing to the hill. There, waves of scarlet and blue blossoms covered the hills. Close by, a waterfall spilled over angular boulders, splashing up on the trunks of oaks. Near them, like a centerpiece, stood a grove of carefully pruned citrus trees, each sparsely laden with large, heavy fruit.

"Your hands have done this?" Risha asked.

Kael smiled. "My hands and elbows and knees and feet, and even my teeth," he responded lightly.

Risha looked toward the marsh of cinnamon-colored cattails with egrets and terns skimming the water. She sang, and her song took wing and carried over the water.

> *The light rushes to the cypress,*
> *to the wood thrush,*
> *to the black swan and dragon eel,*
> *to the roe deer and cheetah;*
> *The light startles my eyes,*
> *Lifts me with wonder—*
> *Wonder at what Aaael has made!*

Kael watched the movements of her throat and lips as she sang of fragrant honeysuckle, minnows flipping in the shallows, a ruby-tailed wasp buzzing a bellflower. She sang humorously of the baggy skin on a flat-tailed gecko and felt Kael's delight suffusing her own emotions.

"Where does it come from?" he asked, his face alight.

"What?"

"The words, the thoughts, the sounds?"

"From Aaael!" She smiled, suddenly amused at herself. "I couldn't stop them, you know. But isn't it the same with you?"

Kael motioned with his hand toward his work. "Yes. But it's a long time since I sprang from Aaael, and I don't hear him as often as at first."

Risha's attention was drawn to an insect on her wrist, half the length of an eyelash and about as thick. It had a narrow, triangular shape. She blew gently at it to make it move. The almost invisible legs, the wings which folded precisely back with streaks of purple and red above the bright green of its body, its *detail,* seemed incongruous for its minute size.

"An incredible miniature!"

"But not half as incredible as you are, Risha." He touched her cheeks and lips with his fingertips.

"Perhaps," she said, "we are the most astonishing beings of all."

RISHA awoke to the songs of meadowlarks and she lay still, eyes closed, listening. This was her second day in the world. When her eyes finally opened, she saw only indistinct light. She blinked, but her vision did not clear.

She stood and passed her hand through the thick mist, and Aaael invited her to walk into it. She felt her way cautiously, sensing the cool moisture on her skin. The morning light in the shifting vapors created movements which made her want to rise up and swirl with them. The mysterious swatching of moisture and light obscured everything but the trees, which loomed up as she walked.

The light began to focus into one source, just above the horizon. She watched the spectacle of the sun burning off the mist, until someone touched her arm and she saw Kael beside her.

"I thought I was in that other world you spoke of," she said softly.

"Sometimes the other worlds touch us unnoticed."

"How strange!" She passed her hand through the mist.

"Strange and wonderful. I've seen things beyond description. Aaael is so much more than a voice and a joy within us."

Risha clapped her hands. "I knew that all along! Aaael told me that. Tell me something I never knew."

Kael laughed a deep, rumbling, infectious laugh which lifted her spirits but perplexed her. "How ancient you are, to know so much," he observed. "Only yesterday, when the sun was eating the mists, you were not!"

She laughed with him then, without embarrassment.

"I'm hungry," Kael said. He picked up a melon and deftly sliced it with the obsidian knife he had made. After they had eaten, he began pruning a plum tree. She watched him for a time, then stretched her arm up beside his to grasp the knife.

She had intended to attempt the work herself, but the touch of her body against his excited her and instead, she looked into his face. He returned her gaze and lowered the knife. But they did not touch again that moment. As an unopened bud is often as beautiful to behold as a full bloom, so the rich sensuality of their light touch and their open gaze fully satisfied them.

Risha sat down at the base of a birch tree to watch Kael work. His thick, flexing muscles reminded her of a school of fat sunfish. As she watched, her back against the tree and her hands upon the partially exposed roots, she began experiencing a new communication. She sensed images of leaves above limbs, and of roots spreading into the earth. The tree was sentient. And not only the tree, she realized, but

14

the grass and the vines and bushes. She detected a unique kind of intelligence; the tree could not reason, but it was aware of all its internal functions, and of all other vegetation.

She felt through this birch tree the oak's sense of height and the coziness of the little strawberry plants at the forest's edge. There was harmony in all their interlocking growth. The oaks allowed the saplings room; vines grew on the trees as adornments to them.

"Kael!" she called. He turned toward her. "I can sense what the oaks are experiencing! Up above the garden and down into the earth. Even your knife upon the branch is part of the harmony!"

"Watch out, or you'll spend the entire morning communing with the plants," he said. "I've done it many times!"

RISHA stood knee deep in water, watching a bird pecking between the teeth of a hippo half sunk into the mud. She was about to wade closer and perhaps climb upon the hippo's back, when a motion caught her eye. She turned toward it to see large, outstretched wings as colorful as that of the ribbon fish. But its movements were swift and darting.

Risha had often been startled in her few days in the world. But no sight delighted her more than this serpent, which hovered lightly above a boulder jutting out of the river, then settled down upon it. The serpent spread its great wings, then gracefully folded them back along its sides.

Risha tried to compare it to other creatures. Unlike the butterfly, which seemed to flutter about aimlessly, the serpent moved alertly, like a falcon. Yet it was like the butterfly in that its beauty was in its wings and colors, and its body seemed a mere connection for the greater glory of its wings. To Risha, its wings looked like thousands of colored dragonfly wings sealed together, translucent, affixed in a marvelous latticework. She had seen no creature with more striking colors and patterns, but size was what set it apart. With wings out-spread, it could have covered a dozen Rishas. Yet, the serpent could fold its wings back around its body, becoming a sleek, supple creature, the rich colors still showing when light penetrated the layers of wings.

Risha walked toward it, and as the river deepened, swam to the boulder, noticing that the serpent's undulating motions were smooth and vigorous, like the movements of the water as it struck the boulder. She put her hand on a crevice and pulled herself part way up.

"You make this boulder into a flower," she said to the serpent, climbing slowly toward it.

"And you awaken all of creation." The serpent's response startled Risha. No creature but Kael had ever spoken.

"You startled me," she said.

"Yes. I felt that," the serpent replied in good humor, for each was experiencing the emotions of the other. She asked him where he had been and where he lived and how it was that Aaael had given him speech and what it felt like to fly. The communion between them was so pleasant that with no hesitation and little forethought, she climbed upon his back. He in turn stretched out his wings and lifted Risha into the air, then hovered and darted along the edge of the river.

They flew far up and then down the river, talking with the breeze in their faces. It was Risha who asked the questions: "Why does that horned chameleon hang by its tail above the water? Why do the fish flip into the air as we pass?" Suddenly, the serpent folded back his wings, anchoring her securely. With her body comfortably nestled behind his head, her face just barely free to the wind, he plunged into the water. Risha soon realized he could swim underneath as agilely as a fish. He wriggled toward the surface with increasing speed and burst into the air in a wide spray. He then plunged deeper and swam along the pebbly bottom.

All manner of fish were attracted. They began swimming about them until serpent and rider exploded out of the water again, circled around, then plunged among them once more. Risha freed one arm to reach out and touch the fish, exultant in the sensation of "swimming" as swiftly as they. The serpent again erupted from the water, spread his wings and darted toward a gnarled sequoia by the garden. He settled on a broad limb and Risha, a bit unsteadily, withdrew from her mount and sat beside him.

Without words, the serpent communicated that his greatest joy would always be in serving her. She had often felt this from various creatures, but it seemed especially pleasing in one who could fly *and* talk and share the wonder of all Aaael had made.

THE seasons in the garden were very mild but unmistakable. Risha and Kael were particularly intrigued by one phenomenon of the cooler season: snow on the top of a mountain. By the time they noticed the small patch of white their first year, it was gone the next day. When they noticed its appearance the next year, Risha said, "Let's find the serpent and fly to see it."

"Why not climb there?" Kael suggested.

They set off, and two black panthers which happened to be with them followed. The first day they walked through level forest and by nightfall were at the slight incline of the mountain's base. They slept there, and in the morning they foraged for nuts as they walked up the steepening slope. Risha watched one of the panthers crush an extremely hard nut between its wide, flat teeth, then efficiently grind it very fine, shell and all, and swallow it. "You have the advantage over us. Here!" she said, placing a nut in the panther's mouth. The animal crushed it and Risha took it from him and ate it.

As they progressed, rock walls rose steeply before them, and Kael and Risha struggled to find handholds. Once, Risha slipped and bruised her knee and scraped her shin badly. She leaned back into a crevice, closed her eyes and directed her body's healing powers to act upon her leg. They rested for a time, then resumed climbing.

Until late afternoon, they helped each other up the steep rocks. Then they found themselves near the top on a gentle slope of earth and grass and occasional cedars. They could see the snow in the distance and began running toward it, to see and touch it before the sun set. Though they ran swiftly, the panthers arrived long before they did. Risha could see them in the distance, pouncing on the white piles and skidding into them, spraying white plumes of snow into the air. When she reached the snow, she imitated them, running beside them, scooping it into the air and kicking it into swirls. The shock of the cold on her hands and feet was refreshing after her long, sweaty run. *It chills like the forest stream,* she thought. *Yet its form is completely different.* She watched as flakes melted on her arm.

"Catch!" Risha called out as she threw some to Kael. They began showering each other with snow and chasing each other as the panthers had.

Slightly chilly, Risha ran into the sunlight, but Kael quickly caught her and tumbled with her into the grass.

Their chasing and wrestling had aroused both of them, and when Kael kissed her, she passionately embraced him. The slow unfolding of their intimacy during many seasons now bloomed like a fully opened rose. Wedded in each other's arms, they whispered of the ecstasy of knowing each other, and the union of Risha and Kael became complete.

18

RISHA walked cautiously, looking up at the stars, her hand probing the darkness for trees and bushes. Night changed her summer forest into intriguing patterns of shadows and odd shapes against the sky. She picked her way slowly, at times stopping to lean against the trees to sense their night moods.

Then she noticed some sort of light at the forest's edge. She thought it was made by fireflies among the marsh grasses and walked toward it. But the light was rolling toward her, shifting, widely diffused, spreading out through the marsh. It radiated blues and greens and golds and seemed to have substance. Risha ran to it, plunged into it, and it swirled around her in a merry dance. She was being touched; the light was thickening and becoming more and more tangible. As she sang out her praise with it, she realized she was moving with a living creature.

Risha kept peering this way and that to see the face of this creature dancing and singing with her. Was it a woman, like herself? No, it was too tall to be a woman; yes, her face looked soft and curved like a woman's; no, its arms were of greater strength than Kael's; yes, her garments flowed around feminine lines and spun about in her ecstasy, even hilarity. Suddenly, Risha stopped and reached out and held the person firmly by her shoulders and looked full into her face.

She felt solid under Risha's hands, but her flesh looked like a form of energy. Her face radiated such a look of joy, Risha could not keep her feet and legs from dancing again. But she held the woman creature fast as she moved, astonished by the face, so much like hers yet so celestially different, a face that seemed about to fuse into colorful, musical light again. "What is your name?" Risha asked, and the light-creature said, "Shia. I am a singer of the songs of Aaael, as are you," and she began a new song about the night creatures of the forest, lifting Risha into the air as if she were weightless.

Risha did not know how long they danced, but she heard many songs from Shia and then suddenly she realized she was singing alone and that the Shia light had become a soft glow in the mountains.

CHAPTER TWO

MANY more seasons passed. Everything continued as in the beginning, with creative labors in the garden, explorations beyond it, and remarkable encounters with other worlds. Risha and Kael spoke often with Shia and other celestial beings; their powers of reasoning and intuition grew.

Risha's delight in being with Kael exceeded all other joys in Aaael's creation. They shared all their thoughts and adventures. One night, as they rested on the grass, Risha told Kael about a perplexing dream.

"I was floating among the reeds on a great beech leaf this afternoon and became sleepy. At first I dreamed of Shia dancing. But then curious beings intruded. They had faces and hands like ours, but they were covered with skins, some like serpent's wings, others like the coats of fawns, and still others like leaves. Their faces had a look of strange rapture as they joined in the dancing, yet their eyes were odd."

Kael rose on his elbow. "What about their eyes?"

"It's hard to say. Bleak, perhaps, or unfocused; but everything changed then. Shia faded away. The music continued, and I tried to keep singing, but the songs no longer came from Aaael. Yet they were lovely sounds which stirred me to rise and watch, and perhaps to worship. Everyone around me—including you, Kael—sang rapturously. We now stood by the hundreds facing a platform high above us, with stairs leading up to it.

"Then an eminence of ruby red appeared above the platform. The light creature shone so brightly I had to put my hand over my face and let its light slowly flow between my fingers. Then more of these beings began to fill the platform. Their hair flowed like a mixture of water and fire. Their arms and legs moved with such grace that the music seemed to come from them. We chanted and danced before them, but, suddenly, everything stopped. From the platform came a purple glow which moved down toward us. I shuddered as it came closer. Not one of us dared look at it, but I glanced sideways at the faces around me. They were still enraptured, but their eyes showed fear.

"The purple light stopped above a person's head, then led him up the stairs. The person chosen wore clothing like thousands of tiny wildflowers pressed together, which hung down in small folds. The light creatures began to create a powerful vortex around him, glittering and bright.

"The ritual went on and on, and when the crashing, driving music and dance were done, a large structure had appeared with white pillars like the trunks of enguila trees. These supported a roof from which tall spires grew. I had never seen anything like it! A crown of light now appeared which floated above the man, then came to rest on his head. At this, all the people below and the creatures above gave a shout, full of triumph and power. As the shout changed into a chant, the man with the crown of light walked toward the white pillars. The purple light went ahead of him, leading him down, down into its maw.

"As the man disappeared, the low chant intensified, and from the light creatures came another fist of color, this time yellow green, which began its descent toward the ecstatic throng below.

"The ceremony repeated itself. But as the second person—a woman—was led with the crown of lights on her head, I found myself beside her, observing her face and eyes. I could never describe the paradox of her expression—ecstatic like the music, yet fearful and alien. The colored fist of light led the woman toward the pillars. At a threshold, she tripped and fell into the building. I could see for less than a second what lay within: shapes of darkness, grotesque limbs.

"But as I was shuddering, I saw another fist of light, this one bronze. It was settling above *your* head, Kael! Then it led you slowly, slowly, as if you were fighting its spell, but drawn to its pleasures—led you to the stairs and slowly up and up. I saw the alien look controlling your face. I screamed against the bronze light, screamed with all my body, but no sound came out. You and the light rose inexorably to the platform, and I stood transfixed above you. I desperately wanted to stop you, but I couldn't move. The living fist of light kept rising. I finally pushed myself into the air and fell on you so that we both crashed among the chanters below.

"I awoke in great agitation, splashing in the water, having fallen from my leaf. It created such chaotic emotions in me, Kael! All my other dreams are pieces of past experiences, but not this one!"

As she had told the dream, Kael's face had tightened and grimaced in ways she had not seen before. Now he said, "I have had three such dreams myself." He lay on his back and looked up at the trees. "I see a person like us, with a regal manner, like the sons of Aaael. Yet his face is disfigured, his eyes impossibly deep set, his jaw twisted. Slowly he turns into a beautiful serpent, the wings so glorious that I long to leap upon him and ride to the skies. But the serpent shrivels, and becomes again the being with the ruined face. Then I awaken and my feelings are much the same as you describe."

Risha sat beside him with her arms around her knees. "But what can we make of such things?" she asked.

Kael was silent for a time. Then he said, "It has to do with the mysteries, the great challenges before us."

Risha smiled and lifted her head. "And we welcome them," she said confidently.

RISHA was watching bees gathering nectar when the serpent flitted past and perched upon a branch. Her spirits lifted. "Where have you been?" she asked.

In response the serpent spread his translucent wings so widely they covered the scope of her vision. "Exploring," he said. Soon she was telling of her own discoveries, including ants which heaped up mounds in the sand nearby and the habits of a marsupial tree frog. The serpent responded with tales of exotic wonders far beyond the river. "Let's find Kael," she said with enthusiam. "He'd love to hear of all this."

"Doesn't he adorn his garden?" the serpent asked. Risha was surprised at the trace of wry humor.

"He adorns it like the center of a flower," she said, but was chagrined at her choice of words, for they didn't seem as clever as the expression on the serpent's face.

"Indeed," was the serpent's only response.

The conversation swept on, and she became increasingly aware that something was changing between them. The talk and laughter were strained; his banter made her feel she had to compete. They never did go to see Kael, and eventually the serpent flew off.

She wondered at the differences in her friend, but shrugged them off and dived from the ledge into the river below. With clean strokes, she swam toward a familiar cave far upstream. Her progress was slow. Not only the fish demanded her attention but also the turtles peering from rocks, muskrats swimming toward her, frogs croaking their greetings. When Risha arrived at the cave, the sun was above her head.

The cave's mouth was edged by split rocks with dark seams of

color. She started climbing toward it, then saw a flash of red in a bush above, like a cardinal flitting from branch to branch. Another, blue like the waters in mid-afternoon, arrested her eye with its quick movements inside the cave. She entered the darkness with her fingers before her, reaching toward the shimmering blue living stone. She moved cautiously until a hand encircled her wrist and began pulling her down, down to the rock floor below the level of the river outside. Long, flowing hair waved before her; it seemed both light and matter, and Risha touched it as they descended. "Shia," she exclaimed, "how can you be both light and flesh?"

"I have taken your form to be with you, but I cannot become wholly you!"

Risha laughed. "No, you are not like me at all, for one moment you are fluid light and the next moment flesh more firm than mine. You change like a tree in the seasons or like water under the sun. You're never the same, but ever a woman."

This time Shia laughed. "I'll try to be more constant in my appearance."

"Don't! Next to Kael, I love you most. I love every changing of you, and every sound and motion! You're the grandeur of Aaael's skies and mountains come to play and sing with me."

Shia sat on a bed of moss and beckoned Risha to join her. "I knew you would come today."

"Yes," Risha agreed. "I need to talk to you."

They watched small movements of color in the depths of the cavern. The living stones were the size of very small birds and could change their colors. Their movements praised Aaael, and their thoughts reached directly into Risha's mind. In reality they were not stones at all but beings from other worlds singing the joy hymns of the universe. One moment the stones would form a shape of spires and towers, another moment trees blowing in the wind, then flashing colors of lightning against the black. Risha found it exhilarating, for their songs flowed through her.

"I had a dream," Risha said to Shia, "of unknown creatures." She related the dream as completely as she could recall it.

Shia did not respond. She sat communing with the living stones around and before her, and Risha saw she was troubled. "This is a warning," Shia said. "It's like Aaael telling you to rise for air from the water's depth, or to grasp the neck of the serpent when you are flying. But this danger is far beyond that of having water smother you—far, far beyond that, which has no ultimate consequence."

The two remained seated on the moss. The songs and motions of the living stones had changed. They were still praising Aaael and his creation, but now the music conveyed a martial mood.

"Recount for me again," Shia asked, "the Visitation. I love to hear of it through your voice and wish to think of it instead of this other. What did you feel?"

"Anticipation. I remember that clearly—the leaves crackled with anticipation. The animals all sensed something was coming. Something *good* was coming, something to feast upon with all our senses. Kael and I were as excited as the animals, waiting with all creation around us.

"Then," Risha continued, "as we sat by the pool at the base of the waterfall, we saw the first of Aaael's children. They appeared as sparkles of light, like stars. But as they drew closer, we saw they were much like us, singing, coming ever closer, finally surrounding the pool and us, their praise almost like laughter. Then they all—there must have been a hundred of them—they all gave a great shout, and it was then that you appeared among them.

"The animals were at first transfixed. Then they joined the music in homage to Aaael as more beings appeared with you, beings I cannot describe at all. We saw light and motion and figures, that's all I can say. We were elated, for we knew that all who led us in this paean of praise had come from the presence of Aaael himself. We fell on our knees, even as we shouted his name."

Risha was so caught up in reliving the experience that she was ready to shout in song again. Shia laughed aloud, bounded up from her mossy seat and sang with Risha, drawing her to her feet.

"And the living stones," Risha called out, "the stones that day, how they sparkled and made such music as I had never before heard nor seen, for they had never been in the world before! And all of this festivity went on and on. We knew we were created for this, and that it was the ultimate joy to praise our Maker with the great ones.

"Indeed!" echoed Shia.

"Then, he came. Aaael came," Risha said more softly. "And it was like a small bird's song after a great wind. Or like the most delicate bloom beside the turbulent waterfall. How can I describe his coming? With words? Simple words to describe Aaael? All my senses couldn't begin to grasp his presence. When Aaael appeared, the event was unmistakable; he had come: Aaael, the holy one.

"His face. You know it, Shia, you know him far more fully than I, his face no one can describe."

As they talked on of the Visitation, Shia expressed much the same joy as Risha did. "No two eyes see a bird just the same," she observed.

"No creature experiences a walk in the forest the same as another. How differently, then, can one experience the presence of Aaael? And how pleasant it is to recount it."

They sat silently, watching the now gentle motion of the living stones before them. "And what did Aaael say to you that day?" Shia asked.

"We are to fill the planet," Risha answered, "first our garden and the lands beyond the forest, and then on and on through all the world. We are to fill it with the fruits of our bodies, with our children and their children. And then we are to fill the worlds of the stars, perhaps the ones you have known, Shia. We are to bring life to the great voids."

"What else did he say?"

"That we are made like him. That we are not merely animals, but are responsible to Aaael. That because of our being like him, we are part of the holy mysteries. That the fruit of the tree at the garden's center is not to be eaten. We have a royal freedom to rule in everything and to enjoy everything, but we are to show our obedience to Aaael through this—never eating the fruit."

Shia rose and stood, looking out the cave's mouth at the sky and water. After a long time she said in a low voice, "Risha, touch me."

The woman stretched out her hand and touched Shia's face. "Risha," Shia said, her voice stern, "in moments of strange thoughts, come to me quickly. Call out to Aaael if you're impeded!"

Risha assured Shia she would do nothing so absurd as to ignore Aaael's warnings. Would she leap from a cliff onto rocks? Would she breathe water? Would she eat stones? Risha laughed. Why would she do something so against her instincts, so absurdly willful?

CHAPTER THREE

RISHA shared with Kael her conversation with Shia. Although the sun was nearly down, he swam with her immediately toward Shia's cave. Shia was sitting outside, waiting for them as they climbed up, dripping, beside her.

The three watched as the sun set and the sky remained luminous for a time, washed with colors, puce, violet, the fading memories of the day's light. Risha then became aware of the stones singing their song of the sun. As the evening darkened and the stars began appearing, their songs extolled the omnipotence behind all spheres, naming worlds one by one and describing their unique glories and the life Aaael had created upon them.

Kael began asking Shia about the dreams, but she didn't answer. She simply motioned for them to follow her up the hill above the cave. There, they came to a little hollow near the forest where they stood under the starlight, silent, until Risha thought she saw a face before her. Then it was gone, but in a moment she thought she saw it again, and a large muscular body beneath it. Shia bid the stones come close, and then Risha saw a masculine face materializing before her, near Kael, rugged jaws and cheekbones, with deep lines and creases in the thick skin. It reminded her of a wind-beaten boulder cracked by the elements. The huge person kept fading, as if having difficulty staying in their world.

"We are at war, you know," the craggy visage said.

"War?" Kael asked.

"The gentle fire which warms and feeds, then devours." The massive face and body disappeared altogether, then suddenly appeared fully visible. "War," the creased lips said, "raises one up, up, up, drawing others along, until at the heights all is reversed, humiliated."

"Didn't I see you at the Visitation?" Kael asked. "You look like one who stood near Aaael himself."

"You did see me," he agreed. "I am Mevorah."

"But we know nothing of war," Risha protested.

The masculine person had seated himself on a rock. Even so, his head was higher than Kael's standing. "Shia and I, and the thousands you cannot see, all of us watch to keep the enemy from you. But he is sly. We don't know what tricks he will use, nor what defense we must bring against him."

"I don't understand," Kael said. "What is to be kept *out?*"

Risha noticed Shia's face contract and it was Shia who responded. "Creatures like us," she murmured. "Great ones of Aaael. Once they were part of us. But not now." Her words were stated with such grief no one talked for a time. At last Mevorah's form began to fade into another world, and he rose suddenly to his feet and moved his arms. At once Risha became aware of thousands of persons barely discernible in glowing white. Mevorah held up his arms and called out a word, unintelligible to Risha, at which the entire assembly formed line on line and looked alertly in their direction. Suddenly the sky was alive with a great crackling of sound and light. Millions of warriors rose with the grace of galloping horses, only far more quickly, and darted around and among the lights and thunders above them so that the din of the noises and the brilliance of the lights caused Risha and Kael to wonder what force could possibly challenge the ultimate power of Aaael.

MORE seasons passed. Risha had been working with Kael on the garden, expanding it so that ingenious networks of plants and blossoms and smaller trees mapped the forest floor. They also tended the tiny plants throughout the garden, maintaining the designs as growth continued.

As they labored in the forest, the serpent came gliding from a tree toward them, and Risha quickly began thinking of clever things she might say. *Why do I react this way?* she wondered, even as her mind searched for appropriate quips. Somehow her relationship with the serpent had changed. He now seemed not only wise, but superior. *Why do I care so much?* she asked herself. The serpent knew things she didn't. Shia knew far more than the serpent, yet Risha never had these strange sensations with her.

"Have you seen the sand in motion, out beyond the forest?" the serpent asked by way of greeting, raising himself to his full, graceful height. His question, had it been from Kael or Shia, would have been a simple invitation to share. But his expression and tone hinted that she had been cheated of seeing some wonder.

"No," she responded, "I haven't even heard of sand like that."

The serpent laughed pleasantly. "Come," he invited, spreading his wings to their full glory. "I will take you there and you can see for yourself."

Kael was planting a bush. "Will you ride with us to see something new?" Risha called out to him.

"When the sun is above our heads, perhaps," he responded, and gave them a wave of both greeting and farewell.

Risha held tightly to the serpent's back. Suddenly its diaphanous

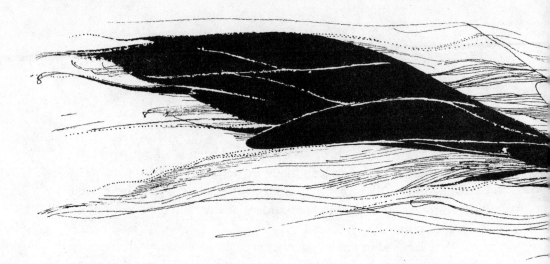

wings beat so rapidly that serpent and rider soared above the treetops. As they flew, she looked down at the forest below stretching out to the mountains. They flew on and on, peaking at great heights and then diving toward the trees, only to soar up again. Finally they came to the other side of the mountains where a desert extended to the horizon. The serpent flew on to angular rock slabs rising abruptly in the desert and landed on a crag overlooking a deep pit.

"Do you see the motion?" asked the serpent.

Risha looked below. Rocks and sand and a gaping pit were all she could see from this height.

"Then let's go closer," the serpent suggested, and winged down to the sandy pit. He hovered over it like a dragonfly and invited her to look down. The depths of the pit were shrouded in darkness, but she saw that the sand surrounding it constantly fell over the edge like a brown waterfall. Dust rose from its edges and filled the air close to it. At first the sand moved sluggishly but then with increasing speed. They hovered so close the dust disturbed her breathing, so they flew back to the crag above.

"Have you ever before seen the sun's rays cutting like rivers through dust clouds like that?" Risha asked. "And how everything's

brown out here—a hundred shades of brown!—except for the blue sky and those sparkles where the sand falls?"

"I've seen other deserts that look purple and then blue-gray as dawn breaks," the serpent said. "There are many terrains that reflect unusual shades of light. But I explore only this world. You've seen far more than I."

"Perhaps."

"I am a mere beast. You are made in Aaael's image. You enter the mysteries of every world. Nothing is withheld from you."

"I love to rise in the morning to see what Aaael will bring to me. But what is withheld from you, that you speak in such an odd voice?"

"Nothing important," the serpent said. He looked at her condescendingly. "But you think something is withheld from you which really isn't. It can make you all you were intended to be."

"Are you playing a word game with me?" she asked lightly. "Your mind is as fast as your wings, but you'll not trick me!"

"I speak of the fruit, of course. The mysteries are waiting for you to grow up."

"The holy mysteries have their own time," she agreed.

"Yes." His smile made her wonder if he had eaten the fruit himself.

She immediately rejected the thought. Surely the serpent, the most beautiful of Aaael's creatures, would not disobey his creator.

The serpent was looking out over the desert, spreading his wings and letting the breeze ripple their edges. Risha said to him abruptly, "I always feel so small after talking to you."

She could not tell how he took her comment, for all the serpent said was, "Yes. Well, it doesn't have to be that way."

"Oh?" she responded.

"Did Kael tell you that Aaael doesn't want you to eat the fruit?" the serpent asked.

"We can eat fruit in the garden," she answered curtly, perhaps the first irritable words she had ever spoken. "It's only the fruit from the tree in the middle we can't eat. We'll die if we do."

"Oh?" said the serpent. He lifted her to his back, then spread his wings to the sky. Almost as an afterthought, as if letting her in on a jest—merely dropping a few words in passing which she had to strain to hear above the wind and the rustle of his wings—the serpent said, "Of course you won't die. Aaael simply doesn't want you to eat it, for then your eyes would be opened. You'd be like him, knowing good and evil."

The serpent did not give her a chance to respond but accelerated his flight back toward the garden. Risha was perplexed by the words "death" and "evil," but she was jolted by his contradicting Aaael. The creator say what was not true? Aaael afraid of her becoming like him? The idea was as silly as hippos trying to fly, or fish walking. Yet the ideas disquieted her.

They landed by the marsh near the garden, and she leaped in among the grasses, splashing and trying to break the mood. A loon came toward her. "Remember," the serpent said in parting, "Aaael wants only the best and highest for you, for me, for all of us. We who are his loyal beasts, and you who are made in his likeness, all of us will

34

find he has far more planned for us than we could ever know. But we must not miss it. We must not miss out on anything!"

KAEL and Risha entered Shia's cave. Deep within, they saw the colors of the living stones and started walking toward them. As they drew nearer, they heard the music of their festivities and began singing with them.

The stones moved toward them, their colors flashing against the cave walls, beckoning to Risha and Kael. Then the stones began to attach themselves to the man's and woman's bodies, covering their skin like jewel-studded garments.

The stones' pulsing penetrated their emotions with unusual sensations. Kael and Risha's frame of reference was changing as the stones sang,

> *You are part of more,*
> *Much more,*
> *And there are more worlds*
> *Than you have dreamed of,*
> *And many ways to enter them.*

They felt transported, past other worlds and into an open hall filled with people singing. The floor seemed made of water, for fish swam below them, yet Risha and Kael stood easily upon the surface. The walls were made of thick moss in which yellow berries were imbedded. The roof was open to the night sky, but neither Risha nor Kael recognized the constellations. They heard a new song now, which came not from any one source. Soon they were singing along, wondering about the cause for the festivities. Neither could later describe the music. It was unknown, as everything there was, yet thoroughly from the heart of Aaael. They found they were floating to the center of the revelers, where they saw a woman on a couch of brown rushes. The woman's body was proud with child and she was singing and clapping her hands with those who were sharing her moment. As the music built to a crescendo, the woman with a great but painless effort pushed the baby out to the world and into the hands of its father. The dance of childbirth ceased as all in the room listened for the voice of the newborn, who greeted them with a fearless cry of life, a cry like that of an exultant child handed a much valued but unexpected gift. The baby continued to give its happy little cries as the mother brought it up to her breast, the umbilical cord still attached. Soon mother and child and father and revelers were all caught up in the dance of completion.

Risha and Kael were then transported from that place to many other experiences on other worlds. When they finally found themselves back at the mouth of Shia's cave, she was there, and she asked them what had happened.

"I'm not sure," Kael responded. "Our experiences were so strange I don't know if they were in flesh or spirit."

"Yet we experienced them together," Risha added, "so it couldn't have been a dream." They compared their sensations and visions as Shia listened, frequently stopping to grope for words. "Somehow," Risha said, "between all these remarkable adventures, we rode upon the vast celestial spaces as you do, Shia, and all of Aaael's arch-regents. We sped through an erupting sun; we felt like comet streaks in a black night. Children of Aaael were all around us, part of a vast harmony. But my words are inadequate."

Shia smiled joyfully. "I was with you all the days of your adventures," she told them, "and Aaael was with us everywhere."

"The wonders of Aaael are always more than I can ever imagine," Risha said.

"You are being prepared for the coming festival."

"Yes, we know it's coming, for Aaael has been whispering to us about it for a long time. When will it be?"

"I don't know, except that it will be at the right time." She paused, then said, "The celebration will be for the child within you."

"But I am not with child," Risha protested, though encouraged by the promise in Shia's words.

"No, but you will be," Shia said, and looked openly from Kael back to Risha.

"Will I know when the seed is growing in me? Will the festivity be like the Visitation?"

"It will be its own event in its own time: the beginning of your task to replenish this earth and others. You shall have many descendants, as many as the living stones, as many as the stars, and a million years from now they will come to you for both your wisdom and your love. Aaael will guide your work, and all worlds shall call you Mother."

CHAPTER FOUR

 MANY days later, Risha sat near the marsh and watched three wispy green insects crawling on the hairs of her forearm. The hairs were so fine she had to bend down to see them, but the little twig-like insects found the hairs like trees in front of them. One got its legs entwined around several hairs which peaked together, and with its stem of a bottom, swayed precariously above her wrist. Risha blew gently at the tiny insect and it tumbled off.

"A humorous little creature," a voice beside her said.

Risha twisted around and saw the serpent, its wings outstretched as if it had just landed. "Yes," she agreed, lifting her elbow so the insect wouldn't fall off. "I don't know if he thinks so. I'd like to shrink down and crawl and tumble with him. But I don't know if it would be so humorous if I were actually that size."

"You'd make him laugh even if he fell on his head." The serpent twisted his own head humorously. "You're the goddess of this world, and everything follows you. Even the large animals, who exceed your size, are like that little insect in understanding and importance."

"But they're as happy as I," Risha said. "They worship Aaael as joyfully as I. So what does it matter?"

"It *doesn't* matter—not at all, not at all," the serpent answered. "I was merely pointing out your greatness, as the moon is brighter than the stars."

"But we have been told the stars are the brighter—they are simply farther away." She felt proud of this slight victory.

"True," he admitted. Risha noticed that the serpent seemed to take pleasure in her little triumph, too. "So the stars are greater than the moon. Aaael has made all things. But he has made some greater than others. And the highest value of all, of course, is *knowing*. That distinguishes you, makes you better than the wolf and the rhino." The serpent rested gracefully on a thick branch laden with blossoms shaped somewhat like dogwood, but yellow with rust-colored imprints.

Risha, who all her life had listened and responded and sung with the voice of Aaael within her, sensed that she should stop this conversation. She thought of throwing a flower at the serpent's face, telling him he was a befuddled but interesting creature, turning from him with a good-natured laugh and running to the ledge and leaping into the water to her aquatic friends below. Yet she also wanted to stay, not wanting to miss anything.

"You breathe like these others," the serpent was saying. "You speak and walk and swim. Yet you are above the beasts as your head is above your feet. Even so, your knowledge is severely limited." He said this last as if it were an afterthought.

"I know all that Aaael has given to me," she responded, "and that is enough—to work and think and speak and sing with his joy."

"Yes—as a grasshopper is happy. But what if you were made to be more than a toad's height above a grasshopper?"

What a strange concept, she thought, to be something other than what she was. She played with the idea. Should she become more than she was now in wisdom and prestige? To have more of the power of *knowing*. It was a tantalizing thought. Discontent, like an alien smoke, began seeping into her emotions.

"Aaael made me. It's silly to think about my knowledge. And

where have you gotten all your insights and splendor?" she asked, trying to sound clever.

"From Aaael, of course." The serpent spread his resplendent wings. "All comes from the good and gracious hand of Aaael—even opportunities he dangles before us, to see if we truly can become great ones."

"You're confusing, and I think perhaps more than a little silly," Risha said. She almost tossed some blossoms playfully at him and leapt away, but she could not quite leave all these unusual thoughts and possibilities, at least for another moment.

"Sometimes one has to *take* from Aaael the good things he provides," the serpent observed with a smile.

"Of course. I take from his hand every day, food and the sweet odors of the field and the water—"

"Did Aaael really say you're not supposed to eat any fruit in the garden?" the serpent interrupted, as if changing the subject.

"I already told you," Risha responded, taken aback, "that we can eat any fruit we want except from the tree in the middle. If we touch it, we'll die."

"You will *not* die," the serpent immediately declared disdainfully, as if sharing something only the initiated could understand.

Why did he bring up this absurdity again? Risha wondered. Aaael had declared something, and this creature of his was contradicting him. It was like saying the sun gave no light. Risha's face twisted in a questioning way, and in response, the beautiful creature gave an elaborate bow, with his wings outstretched along the ground. Risha thought his movement meant he certainly had eaten the fruit and was none the worse for it, but was, in fact, wiser and greater. Was that his meaning?

She continued staring at the intelligent beast. "You won't die at all," the serpent repeated. "Aaael simply knows that when you do eat of it, your eyes will be opened. You'll know good from evil." He stopped talking and ruffled his wings gracefully, looking at her with a bemused expression. Finally, he added, "It really is inevitable, you know."

"What is?" Risha demanded.

"Eating the fruit. What else is to be done with fruit? Would Aaael make it merely to hang there?"

Risha now felt indignant. "No, it is *not* inevitable!" she charged. "The fruit is part of the holy mysteries, part of what already sets Kael and me apart from the beasts of the field. Aaael doesn't play with us, and he doesn't tell senseless riddles."

"Aaael wants only your good," the serpent agreed soothingly. "We all praise him continually, full of joy as we receive all good things from his hand. But surely he doesn't want you to miss something good—not when he himself put the desire for it into you. Isn't the fruit more than delicious food? Won't it also open your eyes?"

The serpent sighed and settled himself comfortably in the sun. "I'm afraid there are but two possibilities," he explained, with an elaborate show of patience. "Either Aaael is not so very good after all, since he would cheat you of this fruit, or he really means to see if you are wise enough to grasp the opportunity. Or a third possibility perhaps. Could it be he's afraid of your taking the fruit? Afraid you may become like him, full of knowledge and wisdom? That you will no longer need him?"

Risha suddenly scooped up a pile of blossoms she had been collecting on her lap and flung them into the face of the serpent, and just as suddenly ran from him toward the ledge above the lake. She did not dive into it but simply ran in full flight over the edge and then plummeted to the water below. She welcomed the refreshing impact and the coolness of the water, but swimming did not dispel the strange ideas. They held a peculiar fascination.

It was several days before the serpent reappeared to Risha. He did so just as she had walked up to the tree at the center of the garden and was staring at the fruit which hung from it. All this time she had pushed the thoughts about the fruit into the back of her mind. She sensed that if she spoke to Kael about it, or went to Shia, they would dispel these ideas as the sun burns up the mist. Yet she was afraid this would mean some sort of loss to her; she could never quite bring herself to speak openly to them about her meetings with the serpent. The growing desire for the fruit lay in her, building power.

The moment she stood before the tree, simply to look at it, the serpent was behind her, watching. The fruit looked succulent, with its skin glistening slightly from the morning dew. She began wondering what its flesh was like. The same apricot color as the skin? Was it as juicy and refreshing as it appeared to be? She began asking herself, Who *did* eat the fruit? She had never seen them lying about, uneaten, around the tree. Did the children of Aaael come in the night to eat them and become wiser still? Was she trespassing on a temple of wisdom reserved for the great ones?

Or was it her right? Wasn't she the favored one on all the planet, appointed with Kael to rule all creatures?

"You will always be a child until you eat the fruit," the serpent said, jolting her by interrupting, yet paralleling her thoughts. "Being a happy baby is all right, but rather confining for the goddess of a planet. I'm a mere beast of the field. But if *you* are to rule the world, you certainly need to know as much as I."

Risha resented this intrusion. She had merely drifted here to look at the fruit and think. But she felt strangely ashamed to dismiss the serpent and she could not bear to hear him laugh at her naiveté.

"I am merely looking at it," Risha declared. "I don't want to change myself from what Aaael made me to be."

"Of course," the serpent agreed. "But a baby tiger outgrows its mother's restrictions. There are mysteries here suitable for one like yourself."

"But I know," Risha admitted, both to herself and the serpent, "that the voice of Aaael within me keeps saying no!"

"Ah!" the serpent responded instantly, interrupting her. "How well I know those voices. Aaael's, yes. But, tell me, aren't *other* voices also speaking to you deep within? Don't they whisper, 'It is inevitable that you will one day eat the fruit'?

"You must not take all this so seriously, Risha. One little piece of fruit? Aaael loves you. Do you think he'd be upset? After all, if Aaael were so stern, why would he allow these conflicting voices to speak to you?"

Risha was discomfited. She would not have called these other signals voices, but, yes, there was something within her which she recognized as the serpent spoke. The voices did tell her she would inevitably pluck and handle and taste the fruit. That the serpent understood this amazed her. The whole experience was so bittersweet she wished she were away from it entirely, racing down a slope with the zebras and wolves, but she could not rid herself of her desires which had little to do with thirst or hunger, but everything to do with this strange compulsion.

"You are vitally alive, Risha," the serpent added. "You can reach for your own destiny as the goddess you are. Others, who have found such wisdom, are clothed in majesty that makes my outstretched wings look drab and my deepest insights seem childish. It's all part of *knowing,* becoming great."

Risha digested this new statement. "So others have eaten the fruit?" she asked.

"In their way."

"And where has it led them? Don't give me these ambiguous answers. What have they found—those who have grasped their own destinies?"

"Freedom," the serpent replied, after only an instant's hesitation. "Freedom from always worrying about restrictions. Freedom to do *anything* they like."

Risha looked at the fruit again, and then up at the sky. "But I already have freedom to do anything I wish, for I want what Aaael wants.''

"Yes, but as I've told you before, you are more than a grasshopper. You deserve at least a taste, a good, full taste of the fruit which will open your eyes. Aaael is not the creator of 'no.' He's the maker of all that delights you. You have childish ideas about him. You might as well pluck it now, eat it now.''

Risha sensed a hint of urgency in his voice. Was something going to happen so that she would not be able to eat the fruit later? Would the temptation be removed after the great celebration which was to occur so soon? This made her even more ambivalent. Would she lose the opportunity to taste the fruit and be wise forever? Or, perhaps, temptation gone, the whole unpleasantness would be behind her?

All this time she had been looking at the fruit on the tree; the fragrance was like a mixture of the choicest apricots and pears. The skin invited her fingers to peel it back to reveal the surely delectable mysteries within. All these abstractions about do and don't seemed irrelevant contrasted with the fruit which was making her mouth water. It looked tangy and cool. The secret was there, and her whole body wanted it. How could something so very good—truly a wonder created by Aaael—be wrong? It seemed so right to be here, looking at this gift of Aaael, yet . . . .

Suddenly, she snatched the fruit from the branch before her and peeled a portion of the skin away.

The flesh of the fruit looked more succulent than any she had seen, a light peach color with a slight purple toward the center. As she tore away a piece, the color darkened into a deeper purple at the pit. She pushed the piece into her mouth. The taste was unique, delicious. She bit into it again, flashes of exotic ecstasy flowing through her, but a strange sense of alarm also tearing at her emotions. Juice ran down her chin; she wiped it off with her fingers as well as she could and turned to look at the serpent. She wanted to say something about this horrible realization which was growing within her, to share the fruit with her ally in this deed. But the serpent had settled himself comfortably under a flowering plum about a stone's throw away, watching, it seemed to her, with a strange disinterest.

Risha wanted more of the fruit. She desired to repeat the initial ecstasy of that first taste. She wanted to lose herself forever in that shocking pleasure that would smother the new voices within her.

She bit into another and quickly ate it, skin and all. But it was not as satisfying as that first taste. She ate another, and then another. As she rapidly chewed and swallowed, a new sensation of continuing hunger and thirst demanded ever more fruit. Always before she had been pleasantly satisfied in eating.

Risha looked again at the serpent, at his detached expression, and this time she understood fully that he had deceived her. Her mouth went dry. She felt rage and horror at the enormity of her deed. She strode over to the serpent, shaking, her eyes tight and burning. "You *lied!*" she spat at him. "You *are* the evil. All that you said were lies!"

"Lied? Not at all. Don't you see clearly now? Didn't I tell you it would turn out this way?"

"I see *you* clearly! I see what I have done against Aaael! You *lied!*"

"Only if you misunderstood. We are allies now, for we have both grown up out of Aaael's cradle, and—"

"Liar!" Risha screamed, and threw herself at the serpent, her hands reaching out toward his eyes. "Evil!" she shrieked at him, but he leaped back beyond her grasp and flew off toward the desert.

CHAPTER FIVE

RISHA stood at the center of the garden, the juice of the fruit still on her fingers and chin, the pits scattered about her feet. Her eyes took in the trees, blossoms, and animals. A pair of chipmunks, chasing each other in a circuitous path, arrived at her feet and chattered for recognition. But her eyes did not waver. Emotions she had never before experienced seeped into her. Alone. Rejected. A traitor among innocent creatures, abandoned by the serpent.

She finally got her legs moving, but she didn't know where to go. She was terrified at the thought of being alone with her knowledge. Kael—he from whom her flesh was made—would he empathize? He couldn't! The bizarre event would repulse him.

Unless he, too, ate of the fruit. Unless he became like her. As she walked, she felt a growing need for him to join her in this dreadful knowledge. To drag Kael into this might be monstrous, yet carrying it alone seemed even more unbearable. Better the guilt of bringing Kael to share evil's enormity, she thought, than to forever cringe under Aaael's wrath alone.

When she found Kael, she smiled self-consciously. She felt extremely awkward standing by him. "You look hungry," she said, reaching out and pulling him away from his work.

Kael returned her smile and let himself be pulled toward her. "You look as if you've started eating," he said pleasantly.

They walked through the garden, eating various fruits from the trees, and seeds from the tall grasses. They chatted amiably as they picked and ate, Risha carefully controlling herself, trying to keep the conversation light. Yet as they walked, she understood more and more fully the immense implications of what she had done. *If I love him,* she wondered, *why do I want him to be as wretched as I?* Yet the terror of her emptiness kept her voice chattering lightly. Finally they stood by the tree which bore the forbidden but enticing fruit.

Kael noticed the pits near their feet. "You have eaten?" he asked, incredulous.

"Yes," she said, maintaining the happy look on her face, all of her willpower keeping her from falling into his arms and sobbing out the truth. They stood in awkward silence for a time. "The fruit is delicious," she told him, "and I have not died at all, as you can well see."

Kael stood still, his face tightly contorted, looking at his mate. Finally he asked, "How could you invade the holy mysteries? Why disobey the command of Aaael? How could you grieve him?"

It took all the power of her mind and body to resist breaking down at his questions. She said, "Why would Aaael make such a delicious fruit if it's not to be eaten? Surely he didn't put it here only to make us want it. Didn't he put desire in us for the fruit? Isn't it simply his way of seeing if we're ready for the greater things? After all, we're the ones with dominion over all who take breath. You—"

Even as Risha presented these arguments to Kael, she realized she was repeating those the serpent had used on her, and she felt nauseated. Yet as she fought the nausea back, her voice and expressions continued the wily dialogue. She led Kael over the same path of objections and counterthoughts as the serpent had. The conversation went on and on. Finally she heard herself using the same urgency as the serpent had on her. She ripped one of the fruits from the tree and held it before him. "How will you ever know, if you don't taste it! Why be cheated of something Aaael has given? Surely you don't think he takes all this as seriously as you do."

Risha had no idea of what was going through Kael's mind as he stared at her. But after a long pause he reached out impassively and took the fruit from her. He bit into it seemingly without emotion, but then she saw in his eyes some of the ecstasy she had experienced at her first taste. As she watched his teeth biting the fruit a second time, she felt both relief and horror. He was now one with her. His innocent face—ah, that wondrous, familiar face of her lover and companion and friend—that face was already starting to change. She stood motionless, expressionless, as he finished the fruit, confirming only with a nod of her head that, yes, it tasted wonderful, and then as he dropped the pit and reached for another, she fell at his feet and began to weep bitterly.

After a time, Kael reached down roughly and pulled her up. It was only with great effort that she made her legs hold steady to stand beside him, but she could not raise her eyes, could not face him after what she had done to them both. *But he is as guilty as I,* she repeated to herself as she stared at a pit lying sticky in his hand. *He succumbed to precisely the same temptation, and we are equally renegades.* Her face felt puffy and wet, but as she looked at Kael she saw his face was no less alien than hers to all they had known before. *I listened to my serpent; he to his,* she thought. *Ah, bitter! Bitter!*

No words passed between them as they stared at each other in their mutual humiliation. She reached out and touched his face tenderly, contritely.

"Let's go to the water and wash," he said, his voice flat. They walked to the river and kept walking until they were neck deep. Their hands began scrubbing against the sticky sweetness on their faces, scrubbing angrily at the juice wherever it had dripped on them. They continued vigorously cleansing themselves, repeatedly splashing and rubbing, then emerged from the water to stand under the hot sun, wet and dripping. She looked at the man beside her; pain was beginning to etch new lines on his face. Her sense of Aaael's presence was gone; she felt self-centered, the expansive feelings of the universe now replaced by a compacted sense of foreboding.

She noticed a deer moving in the garden. She looked at her body, then Kael's. They were both naked. What an odd, fearful sensation. It grew within her, this conviction she should not be seen, and it shocked her into dipping down into the water to be covered. Yet the water was translucent.

"We must find a covering," she said, shame drawing blood to her face as she moved quickly to a nearby clump of bushes. Kael followed and took charge of fashioning rude loin coverings from the leaves, his silence adding to Risha's fright.

As she reached with shaking hands for the leaves and pulled them from the branches, she felt only the leaves' smooth skins. Her old communication with the trees had been cut off, like sunlight behind clouds. She felt isolated, even from Kael. Her seducing him to eat the fruit had done nothing for her.

They stood among the thick bushes, feeling rather foolish with the leaves draped around them. Where were they to go? What were they to do?

Aimlessly, they started walking toward their bower. Risha gritted her teeth. She expected the animals to come rushing up to her when they saw the leaves on her, anxious to play whatever new game she had thought up. She would be embarrassed. But no squirrels came scampering, no horses came nor wolves nor bluejays. She looked about as she walked and noticed that an elk at the edge of the forest was looking at her. Was there a wariness in his stance, in the cock of his head? Beside him in a tree was a white owl, and she imagined that it looked down at her in outraged judgment. How could any of this have happened, she wondered, just from eating some fruit? Had that one act split the core of Aaael's creation and changed everything?

The animals remained distant as Risha and Kael began walking

52

awkwardly toward the bower. She noticed a hawk gliding above the garden. Suddenly it plummeted to earth, but almost immediately it rose with something in its grasp. Was that a mole it held limp in its talons? *What's that all about?* she wondered. Risha looked at Kael, who had seen it, too, but neither spoke. They walked on, and in the bower dropped upon their soft bed. Another phenomenon was starting in their bodies, a tension and weariness which did not simply invite sleep but made them irritable.

Both lay there, resting and thinking. As the sun lengthened the shadows of the trees, Risha several times reached out and touched Kael lightly, but he did not respond. What raged in him she could only guess by what she felt. She found it an awful thing to be awake in the universe.

She rose from their bower and without looking at Kael, walked out to the ledge high above the lake. Behind her were the same banks of blossoms, but she had no inclination to pluck them. She had thought she might leap down and swim among her aquatic friends, but as she stared down the great distance, she felt afraid. The assurance that nothing could go wrong because of Aaael's voice within her was gone. She looked at the empty garden. Despite the leaf coverings about her loins, she felt naked.

Risha stepped back from the disturbing height and retraced her steps through the garden. She saw antelopes in the distance scurry away from her, and she wondered as she watched them flee if they felt the same fear she did.

When she stood in the bower once more, she reached down her hand to Kael and invited him to stand. "Let's visit Shia and ask her what to do," Risha said. "She has always loved us, and maybe she'll comfort us." Risha sensed her words were stilted, even as her touching Kael was awkward, and she had no assurance Shia would comfort them at all. But Kael nodded and rose. As they walked slowly through

GDEVELASCO © 80

the garden, she wondered what was going through Kael's mind as he saw no animals.

Their long swim to the cave was equally eerie, for they had never splashed into the water before without being greeted by their fellow creatures. They pulled themselves from the river at the cave's entrance and climbed up the slabs of rock. They saw no living stones in the dark belly of the cave. Again, nausea affected her as they walked in for a short distance, feeling the rock edges, and continually turning to look at the light behind them.

They heard a sound, a slight shifting of rocks on the floor, as if someone had moved a foot. "Who are you?" Kael demanded. Risha grasped Kael's arm. No answer came, but two hands grasped a shoulder of each of them and slowly led them back to the light at the entrance. Risha realized it was Shia who guided them, but her touch was not the same. As they stopped at the entrance and the sun illumined her face, Risha felt devastated. Had she caused what was in Shia's face?

Risha's guilt almost buckled her knees, but then, suddenly, she was indignant, with a rage so uncontrollable it seemed to come from outside her. "Your eyes accuse me, Shia!" Risha said sharply. "The horror of all this descends on me with no mercy! Where were *you* at the crucial moment? If so much depended on my one small act, why didn't you tell me? How could I know all those words were lies, I who had never been lied to, never before, *never!* Why didn't you tell me—"

"You were told," Shia interrupted, just as sharply. "You were told that if you ate of the fruit you would surely die."

A chill of new fear struck Risha's body. "I have not yet died," she responded weakly.

"Is this not death?" asked Shia. She waited as the full force of the words hit the woman. "There is more, far more to come," she warned. "Your glory has departed."

"It's more than we can bear!" Risha said fiercely. "Didn't Aaael put curiosity into me? Where was he when my hand reached for that accursed fruit?"

"It was not accursed," the voice from the grieving face corrected. "Who knows what joyous purpose it may have been to you? Perhaps in the great festival, you would have been invited to taste, the great festival which now shall never take place."

"Agh!" Risha screamed. "How can all, all, be changed? Where were you when the serpent tempted me with his lies? Where was Aaael? His silence has murdered us!"

"Risha! I was here. I was *always* here. When you were troubled, did you call out to me? Did you call out to Aaael? You were free, the heiress of all creation. Aaael loved you enough to let you choose. Wasn't your heart's desire to eat the fruit? You didn't *want* my presence, nor Aaael's. He remained silent to give you your choice. If he hadn't, you'd be merely a beast of the field, a frog or a hare—"

"Better a hare!" Risha shouted. "Better a slug! Better a worm!"

"No! You were created to be more. When you were made, the stars sang together, and all the children of Aaael shouted for joy. His love bade you to choose him, and if you had, your greatness would have been secured."

Risha's eyes moved toward Kael's face. His silence added to her humiliation. He was standing impassively, staring at Shia.

"We are at war," Shia added, "and you have embraced the enemy."

Risha ignored the accusation, desperately trying to rescue herself from this maddening discussion. "What is this incredible business of Aaael's great ones falling? Why tell us these tales? They're mysteries beyond simple ones like Kael and me. If creatures like you can become fiendish liars who change everything into death and fear, why should we have to disbelieve those clever lies? Why were these fiends unleashed on us? Would I blame a rabbit if I lured it over a cliff?"

Shia did not answer, but Risha saw in her face such a longing for them that she could keep up her outrage no longer and started weeping. Shia then gathered both the man and the woman into her arms and wept with them, kneading their shoulders with her fingers, whispering, "My little ones. My little ones. How you have grown past me and fallen."

And then Shia was gone and they were left at the entrance of the cave, wrapped in each other's arms, silent.

Suddenly Risha ran into the river and began swimming back toward the garden. She swam furiously, spraying the water widely around her. When she rose on the shore of the garden, she felt numb. All that she saw was Aaael's—trees, sun, water, earth. Yet she felt cut off. Even that rebellious, beautiful creature, the serpent, was made by Aaael. What wretched mysteries! The very stillness and beauty of creation mocked her.

She picked some seeds and ate them, then climbed to her ledge above the river. She was there for several hours before she heard in the distance shrieks and grunts and a feline spitting sound. The noises increased as she ran down the hill toward them, and then she saw a bear burst from the forest with a tiger chasing it, snarling and spitting. It was one of the grey bears, eyes near-red with fury. As the bear turned to protect itself, one of the tiger's cubs approached from behind. The diversion gave the tiger the instant it needed to leap at the bear's throat, snapping its teeth shut upon it and clawing wildly with its hind legs. The bear's claws raked the tiger's black-and-gold coat, drawing wide streams of blood. But the tiger's hind feet were clawing and digging at the bear's belly, ripping out intestines. The bear screamed horribly, and the tiger leaped free. The cub spat at the bear and moved closer to worry him, but with a tremendous effort the bear moved its body and swung its paw in one motion that caught the tiger cub behind the ear, splitting its skull.

The tiger, seeing its cub dead, snarled in rage but stayed out of range of the bear's claws as its dying enemy kept swinging and roaring.

It took a very long time for the bear to die. Risha stood transfixed, learning of death and what the insides of creatures were like, ripped open, steaming and contracting eerily in the air. At last the bear was dead; the cub lay beside it.

She looked at her friend the tiger, long streaks of blood on its back. The beast's eyes were changed, inscrutable. She turned her head. The tiger's mate was near, moving its eyes from Risha to the dead cub, back to Risha, back to the carnage. Risha again felt fear, but this time a visceral fear. Could her body be mauled like that? Was this the death prophesied for her?

The great cats stood staring, imperious. Did they know she had caused all this? She wanted to run, to fling herself from the ledge into the water. Although fear of the tigers rushed through her body, she almost wanted the animals to slash her, to avenge themselves and all creation, so that it was her blood soaking into the ground.

But they did not. Both slowly, it seemed interminably, sniffed the bodies of the bear and their cub. Then, with a last mysterious look at Risha, they padded quietly into the forest.

Slowly Risha advanced toward the bodies. Death. It was like sleep. But the blood! The viscera! The screams! She knelt by the cub. Suddenly she dropped down, lay beside the cub and hugged it tightly against her, sobbing. She lay there for a long while, holding the soft-furred body. Images passed through her mind of her own death, and of Kael's. The bear's head lay in a clump of yellow flowers which contrasted grotesquely with the blackening blood.

Then she began sensing a little of her old communication with the plant world. The grass and a beech tree her shoulder leaned against were communicating something, but she had to use all her powers to pick up their distant concern. As she concentrated, she realized the unnerving truth. The only reason she could sense their communication was that the grass roots and tree roots were screaming. Screaming against defilement. The blood of the animals had reached them and was being drawn in. They cried out against the blood, against this desecration.

Risha heard only faintly the scream traveling through the forest, through the grasses and seedlings and vines. The message traveled through all vegetation of the planet, like a great chorus with only one anthem:

Fear. Fear. Fear.

The great harmony was lost. Chaos was loose.

She lay there until she could sense the cries from the trees and plants no more, as if an explosion had rocked down a canyon and then echoed into silence.

CHAPTER SIX

 RISHA was still thinking about the killing she had witnessed when Kael entered their bower and sat wearily, but also warily, beside her. She looked at him; there was a wild expression in his eyes. "Aaael is coming," he said, rubbing a pile of straw between his palms. "He's coming himself." He did not elaborate, nor tell why he thought Aaael was coming.

The fear she sensed in him increased her own. She longed to be reconciled, at least to Kael, so that they could face what was coming together, but she saw no way to penetrate his anger. *If he feels toward me what I feel toward the serpent,* she despaired, *there is no hope whatever.*

"Death has entered the garden," she said to him. "Did you see it as you came?"

His head jerked toward her. "What do you mean?"

"The tiger and the bear clawed and ripped each other. The bear lies dead; so does the tiger cub."

"How does this death change them?"

"Go and see. They are by the tiger's lair."

He did not move.

"They lie there as if asleep, though torn and gouged. Kael!" she screamed suddenly, "what will they loose upon *us* if we are to be ripped and still like those creatures?"

Kael did not answer. Eventually he rose, said that he would look at this death, and departed. Watching his back recede along the trail and recalling his frightened face intensified her apprehension even more.

Aaael himself! How will I stand before him? I'll grovel into the cracks in the earth. Right now he knows where I am. Why does he prolong my terror?

The sun was starting to go down and it was becoming cooler before Kael returned. She felt his hand jerking at hers, the fear in his voice as well as his face. "He's here! In the garden!"

Risha found herself running with Kael toward the forest, trying to escape, scurrying past the larger bushes so they would not be seen. She saw no signs of Aaael's majesty, none of his magnificent children.

They cowered under thick bushes among the trees, and as they sat, hushed and still, Risha could hear Aaael walking. Then they heard his voice, which pierced Risha like a knife. "Kael," the voice summoned, "where are you?"

Kael hesitated, then looked at Risha and back in the direction of the voice. He set his face into an inscrutable mask and moved toward Aaael with uncertain gait.

Risha moved surreptitiously behind him, staying hidden in the bushes. "I heard you walking, and I was frightened because I was naked," Kael said. "So I hid from you."

Risha looked at Aaael. His eyes held all the glory she had seen in the Visitation. It was the mark of Aaael's ultimate grandeur that he could compress all of that into the form of a man—as if all the stars and novae had fused into one man-sized creature. He wore a white garment which covered all but his head, his hands, and his feet.

"Who told you that you were naked?" Aaael was demanding of the man. "Did you eat from the tree I commanded you not to eat from?"

"The woman you put here with me—*she* gave me some fruit from the tree, and I ate it," Kael said.

The words and the guilt burned into Risha, and Aaael turned and stared at her, as if he had seen her during every moment and knew her every thought. "What have you done?" Aaael asked.

Risha stood now before Aaael, and the words came to her tongue involuntarily. "The serpent lied! He lied and lied to me; he deceived me . . . and I ate."

Aaael did not respond to this, but turned and moved his arms. In the distance Risha could see a speck of color which began growing larger. Then she saw as it came closer that it was the serpent. The graceful creature bowed submissively before Aaael and looked expectantly, yet coolly, toward his maker.

Aaael declared, with anger, "You are cursed! You will crawl on your belly and you will eat dust all the days of your life!"

At that, the serpent's great wings spread out and their translucent colors began to darken and the wings themselves shriveled. The thin membranes of those wondrous designs peeled and curled as if touched by fire, and the frames shrank smaller until the wings became mere scabs upon his body.

But what happened to his face and torso seemed to Risha macabre. His body began stretching out, longer and thinner, and the face became a long, fanged parody of the original. Ever afterward Risha would think of this transformation as perhaps the greatest horror of all, for it seemed to typify what had happened to everything she had loved. The serpent was still the same creature, but as grotesque as he had been beautiful.

She shuddered as she saw the serpent now squirming and wriggling in his unaccustomed state, with that new fanged face which looked at her with hatred, as if her words alone had brought him to this fate. "Serpent," Aaael now stated, "I will put hatred between you and the woman, between your children and hers. Her child will crush your head, and you will strike his heel." Risha stared at the writhing, enraged serpent, and her revulsion centered on the image of crushing that head, and she longed to do so now, right now; she caught herself looking about on the ground for a rock.

But Aaael turned to her and said, "When you bear children, I will greatly increase your pains. Your desire shall be for your husband, and he will rule over you."

And then Aaael was speaking to Kael about the ground being cursed and that thorns and thistles and sweat would be his lot until they both returned to the ground. Relief rushed into her, that at least they would not be ripped apart. At least their blood would not drench the roots of the grass this day. How they would return to the ground she did not know, but somehow it mattered a great deal that it not be now.

The serpent started wriggling its way toward the forest, awkwardly humping and twisting. Aaael ignored him and motioned the man and the woman to follow. Aaael walked toward the lair of the tiger, with Risha and Kael behind him, numb in their chastisement. At the bodies of the cub and the bear, Aaael knelt and pulled a long, thin knife from under his garments. Then he methodically made an incision in the shoulder of the bear.

Risha, with Kael, looked on in stupefaction as Aaael sliced the white, fatty tissues, separating them with quick, deft strokes. In a day of bizarre wonders, what could this mean? Aaael himself, maker of all the universe, kneeling on the blood-stained grass and cutting away the skin from his slaughtered creature? If the eating of the fruit was such a horror, how could the holy Aaael do worse by desecrating these animals?

But as before, when Aaael had spoken to her within, the answers came as he skinned the bear, blood soaking into his sleeves and grease upon his hands. He was doing all he could for them. The enemy had won and could claim his due and his curse. Blood and death and nakedness were now realities. But Aaael would be with them, even in the judgments he pronounced—in the sweat of the brow, the pain of childbirth, the unthinkable tasks of slicing up a body.

But we have been cursed! Risha cried out within herself. *How can you be with us?*

No, Aaael's voice seemed to say, *in my wrath I cursed the serpent first. The ground and the serpent have been cursed, but not you. You must bear only what you have brought upon yourself, and through blood and pain and repentance—*

Blood and pain and repentance; the words struck a chord of anger within her. Repent? Pain. Repent? Blood. Why was it all laid on her? She watched as Aaael continued to skin the bear, but his thoughts no longer mingled with hers, though she longed for them to do so even as she resented them.

While Aaael was skinning the bear, night fell, but thousands of the living stones hovered close and provided a light of varied colors. He finished the task, leaving the carcass on the ground, the unskinned paws and face contrasting with the white body, ghastly to Risha's eyes. Aaael then turned to the tiger cub's body. Risha hated seeing the knife enter the skin and to see it start to peel off, leaving the white and pink flesh beneath. The cub could not be feeling any of this, Risha thought to herself. Otherwise, Aaael would have nothing to do with such a deed. The cub is surely beyond all pain, and perhaps that is what Aaael is trying to teach us.

Aaael pulled the small tiger skin from the carcass and then held out the wet, fleshy side. Risha could see that his hand held burning flames, which turned the skin brown and dry. He did this to both skins, then took his knife and carefully fashioned them into sets of simple clothes. He placed them on the man and the woman; they fit perfectly.

Then Aaael bade them sleep, and the stones hovered around them, as if to watch over their troubled thoughts.

Both Risha and Kael dreamed all through that first night, but neither could recall their dreams. Both man and woman felt stupified, lying in their bower, occasionally rising to eat some seeds. The living stones remained around them until Aaael returned when the sun was above their heads. His face still showed enormous grief, and he motioned for them to walk toward the forest. He went before them, through the garden, and finally to the edge of the high oaks. Then Aaael stopped and looked at them. He said nothing, but before him appeared a flaming sword as large as Kael himself, turning back and forth, issuing an inexorable warning.

Aaael turned without speaking and walked back into the garden. Risha was dismayed, and shivered, though covered by the warm skins.

Kael grasped her hand and led her deeper into the forest. He stopped and picked up some nuts, cracked their thin shells in his hand, and shared them with her. They went on and finally reached a clearing where they sat down, looking numbly at the forest around them. Sunlight slanted past the trees and into their clearing; they soon became drowsy and lay back in the grass.

As she put her arm over her eyes to try to escape into sleep, her mind was like the rapids of a river, splashing in one direction, then another, roiling, chaotic. One idea she began exploring started a pleasurable burning in her belly, which moved up into her throat and then to her eyes which began to water slightly as she let this bittersweet emotion well up. *Unjust!* she thought. *Why am I here? I have loved much. I always have. Aaael, how can I accept this?*

The sun's rays broke through the leaves, forming a mottled pattern on her skin, but she was unaware of the light shifting. She began dreaming about the living stones, only this time they did not seem full of music and joy, but of anger and judgment. Then she dreamed she was in her garden, trying to protect it and all its creatures from the stones. But she saw eventually that the stones did not attack her or her animals, but simply faded away and she was alone in the garden.

The tiger came to her, full of his old playfulness, and both its cubs came and romped with them, and Risha wept in relief. She jumped from the ledge, her arms full of blossoms, and the tigers leaped with her, plunging into the water, but then urging her to the shore as aquatic creatures began their gambols with her. But as she sported with them, an icy breath blew into the world. She had just been rising naked from the water when its chill hit her wet body so forcefully that she crouched for warmth. The tigers, too, felt it, and began snarling and spitting, and their actions became bizarre. They leaped nonsensically, irritably.

The icy, fetid breath blew against her. It shriveled the plants and maddened the animals still further.

Then came the apparitions, cold shapes stalking her. At first she could make nothing of them but shifting shadows darting among the trees and bushes. Yet as they came closer, she saw glimpses of shrouded faces. No, not faces, but skulls with meat on them, battered noses, low-slung jaws, penetrating eyes. Arrogance glowed from those eyes, staring at her in condescension. The eyes were stuck within empty skull sockets and turned this way and that, fixing upon her hungrily.

These dark specters whirled now throughout the garden in complete control. But then she saw Mevorah enter the garden, glowing in all his strength so that the specters fled. In his hands Mevorah held a large, rough-hewn cup made of wood. He stood before Risha, the cup in his hands, and to her horror she saw that the specters were being forced, howling and spitting and wailing, into it. Then she saw other putrefactions squirming and tumbling and oozing into the cup, until she thought surely it must be filled many times, but still more came, until at last Mevorah raised his hand and stemmed the flow, saying, "It is enough."

He stood before Risha then, for what seemed to her years and years upon years. The cup before her. The cup of Risha. The cup she had brought to herself. *Yet haven't I already drunk it!* she screamed within. Mevorah put it gently into her hands and she stood there with the

weight of it seeming to bear her to the ground, repulsed by what she saw within, wriggling and howling and lashing their terror toward her. She tried to lift it to her lips but could not.

Then she saw in the far corner of the garden a light. It was a figure walking toward them. As he came closer, she saw that he was clothed in light, as if the light had substance and flowed gracefully from his body.

Then Risha saw his face, and she knew it was Aaael. His face transfixed her, that indescribable expression of love, holiness, grandeur. She collapsed to her knees, the vile cup still in her hands, her eyes focused on his face.

Aaael said nothing. He continued to look down at her. Then he slowly lowered himself to his knees before her. She saw in his eyes the same suffering she had seen on Shia's face. She was terrified.

Aaael reached out with his eyes still on hers and asked her to give him the cup. His voice was like the sound of the ocean against the cliffs. He took the cup in his hands and raised it slowly, slowly, not to her lips as she had thought, but to his own. He held his eyes on hers, and the grief was awesomely clear on his face as he tipped the cup and drank. It seemed that he drank forever, drank all of it. She could smell the stench and see the slime at the corners of his mouth, but still he drank!

She panicked. She felt she was pouring the filth into Aaael's mouth herself, but she couldn't cry out.

Finally Aaael set the cup down, and reached out for her and raised her to her feet. His hand, though glowing light, was soft as any flesh; his eyes penetrated her spirit.

Then he crushed the cup under his foot.

CHAPTER SEVEN

THE smoke from the fire was blowing back into their cave, but Risha could do nothing to stop it. She shut her smarting eyes and put on another log. She could not let the fire die with Kael and Erlin, her son, suffering from fever on damp skins. The cave smelled of perspiration and vomit.

She muttered aloud, moving with weak, unsteady motions. She had barely recovered from the sickness herself. She looked at her son. The morning light was filtering in and illumined Erlin's young, lightly-bearded cheek.

Death. Risha had learned to despise its frequent presence. Three days ago, in the throes of the sickness herself, she did not care if it took her. But now Erlin, who loved her most, this center of her life, shivered on the edge of that stillness and decay. "I will follow him," she thought bitterly. "If he goes, I will follow him!"

Onar, her elder son, appeared in the doorway. "You'll have to take the flocks and tend the traps," she directed him. "Where have you been?" Her question sounded like an accusation.

"Sleeping on rocks is better than smelling this all night," Onar said.

"You might have been needed," Risha countered, her face as tight as a goatskin drying in the sun, "if only to ease their dying."

"They won't die! You haven't; they won't."

Risha started, amazed. Did his inflections imply he wished she had died? No, that thought was her own anger bleeding through, and if her tone of voice accused him of that, she would be even angrier with herself. Risha often sensed she was driving her older son from her. Now, she tried to remain strong, without letting her rancor show. "You must tend the traps and care for the sheep," she commanded.

"But you've already ordered me to keep fuel for the fire, and my field work exhausts me. Remember, I lived through the sickness, too, and no one did my work."

"No animals hung trapped in the forest waiting for you," Risha retorted. "No flocks bleated from hunger."

"You see," he said, as if she had just entered his trap, "my work is frivolous. It can always wait. The *real* work is Erlin's and yours, and my father's." Onar looked down at the shivering forms. "I recovered. They will, too."

"Onar," Risha said angrily, "you're only trying to provoke me. You know we couldn't live without your work. But go. I'll tend the traps and flocks myself. Only mind you, keep piling up fuel, and don't let the fire go out!"

Risha walked in the refreshing cold air to the ravine about a mile away where the goats were penned. Two logs standing on end kept them blocked in. Each log was about the thickness of her waist, and heavy. She grasped one at the bottom and laboriously pulled it up so that its base rested on the rocky ground beside the hole. Then she let it fall outward. It hit with a loud thud, which sent the goats off in a clatter of hooves to the far slope.

Fear. Always the fear, she thought.

Most of the goats were brown with black markings and streaks of white on their faces. She studied the constant twitching of their skin against mosquitoes and gnats as they walked warily around her to the opening.

Once past her, they ran through the narrow aperture to the closest grass and bushes. She came up behind them and started herding them toward the river and the traps. It would be difficult, herding and trying to check the traps at the same time, but she had to make the best use of her time and strength.

The first trap was a vine set to snare an animal's foot. It remained empty and waiting, with not even a track nearby. She moved on to another, driving the goats around it. From a distance, the second trap looked sprung and empty. But as she drew closer she saw a rabbit's hind foot dangling at the end of the vine. Something had eaten the snared animal; a fox perhaps. She tried not to think of it dangling there as the predator approached. She tossed the foot away and reset the trap.

The goats were intent on feeding and she switched at them to get them moving. It was nearly noon when she finally found a snared animal. The rabbit was in the middle of blue-green grasses where a clump of slender, white birches grew. It dangled by its hind foot, and Risha looked at it with compassion. How long had it been hanging there? An hour? Two days? She hated the traps.

Risha walked swiftly to the rabbit, which began to jerk its entire body in panic. Not until her hand grasped it on the back did it let out that loud, unnerving squeal she so hated to hear, and she swiftly brought the club down upon the base of its skull to silence it. She cut its throat and then began dressing it, the warm viscera spilling out on the ground, the kidneys like small red stones surrounded by white fat.

Eviscerated, the rabbit now hung from a vine around her waist. She moved on. How strange, she thought, that all of this had become her natural pattern, hunting, trapping, eating animal's flesh, tearing their skins from their warm bodies and placing them on her own.

The last trap had snared a beaver. A beaver with its excellent pelt and nutritious flesh. The sight of this larger animal hanging upside down disturbed her. She strode to it quickly, anxious to have the deed done. The beaver snapped at her and twisted angrily on the vine, but she clipped it a heavy blow, a blow full of her anger at having to do this, and it stunned the animal long enough for her to strike it fatally behind the head.

As she made a slit from its throat down the center of its belly, she noticed under its arm a kernel of ripe corn. She reached to pick off the yellow kernel but it seemed stuck. She pulled harder, but it was fastened to the animal's skin. Irritated, she grasped the little object firmly between her fingers and pulled with her whole might. The kernel finally popped away from the beaver's skin, and she turned the little object around in her fingers. Then she saw the wriggling feet at its base.

"Parasite!" she said with disgust, tossing it far from her.

Barking dogs interrupted her. She began to run toward the bleatings of the herd. When she reached them she saw immediately that the dogs had succeeded in their strategy. They had separated a mother goat and her two kids from the rest of the herd, forcing them to the center of a field where she could not effectively protect them. The mother goat whirled and charged at one dog, then twisted quickly to ward off another. The young kids tried to stay close to their mother, but she was tiring.

Risha dropped the beaver and rabbit carcasses and ran toward the pack, screaming and brandishing her club. The dogs were not large, and at the sight of her they snarled but started backing away. The mother goat quickly bounded toward the herd, her two little charges racing behind her. Risha threw rocks at the dogs, and she felt pleasure at hearing one yelp.

Risha walked among the goats, patting them reassuringly, then returned to where she had dropped the beaver and rabbit. The rabbit was gone, stolen by the dogs, she supposed. She spat angrily upon the ground, hoisted the beaver to her side and started herding the goats home.

Chasing the stragglers through the aperture into the ravine nearly exhausted her. The bout with the fever had left her weak; lifting the logs and dropping them into the holes made her body shake.

As she walked toward the mouth of the cave she saw that no light flickered within. Not even smoke wafted into the twilight. She forgot her weariness and strode quickly into the cave and to the two forms upon the skins. The fire was barely flickering; both men still breathed. She hurriedly dropped the carcass to the floor and walked out to the stand of trees some distance away. She saw no loose brush or dry limbs so hurried on into the forest. Her rage began to replace her fear for Erlin and Kael as she contemplated her hardships of the day and Onar's failure to follow her orders. *He could easily have checked the traps,* she thought, *while I could have been tending Kael and Erlin.* By the time she returned to the cave and had the fire going, she was moving with a cold, calculated fury.

Onar eventually entered with an armload of wood and walked over to the fire. He began carefully laying the logs on it. Risha did not greet him, but stared, her face frozen and her eyes intent. Onar brushed his hands against each other to wipe off the scraps of bark and other debris, then began to walk out. He was already past Risha when she accused him, her single word like a stone cast against flesh: "Parasite!"

He turned to face her, but said nothing. He stared at her, then walked out into the twilight.

He returned with another armload of wood and dropped it with a crash beside the fire, then went out again and reappeared shortly with more wood. He rapidly dropped his burden, turned on his heel and left again. As he brought yet another load of wood to add to the growing pile, Risha screamed, "Onar! I'm speaking to you. I'm outraged that you would leave Kael and Erlin with no fire!"

"Parasites do such things," he replied.

"Yes!" she agreed caustically. "Don't walk away! You are as responsible as I for your father and brother. They could have died!"

"Mother," Onar declared, biting his syllables off as if they were bits of meat, rising up to his full, muscular height, "I haven't ignored anything. I left them with fire for the long day, and all this time I've been gathering wood. To get dry pieces I had to go a long way."

She realized she had misjudged the situation, although she still considered it inexcusable to have let the fire die. But nothing would allow her to reach out to him in apology. "You were told to keep the fire going," she insisted, never changing her rigid expression.

Onar did not reply, but glared at her, then brusquely walked out.

Risha kept her body moving through her tasks, pouring the leeks and goat-neck soup into a clay bowl and letting it cool, continuing to tend the fire, eating some of the soup herself directly out of the pot. She fed Kael, getting perhaps a few spoonfuls into him. Then, as if saving the most welcome task for last, she stooped and cradled Erlin's head on her lap and placed some of the warm fluid between his lips. Erlin. He would never speak to her as Onar had. He would never cause her pain as Onar did. Perhaps she provoked Onar at times, but from his early childhood, beginning with Erlin's birth, Onar had turned mean. He would torment Erlin, and trick him in their games with stones and feathers.

Erlin. She spooned more of the liquid between his lips and gently rubbed his ear and hair, as she had when he was small enough to sit on her lap. He had always believed absolutely in Risha's promises that they would return to the garden some day.

Why was Onar so disagreeable? She remembered well the pain of his birth. In fact, during its peak, she had thought this was how she would die, fulfilling the prophecy. But she remembered even more her elation at bringing forth her first child and of holding him close to her. She had cried out her thanks to Aaael, for she was convinced this was the child of promise who would somehow bring about their reconciliation with Aaael. That first year of seeing Onar change in

abilities every week had entranced her. Everything about him was new. During the following years she had been fascinated by this person who had come from her body. She had loved him, and even in the hardest days of toil had found times to caress him and laugh at his antics.

But when Erlin had been born, Risha's heart had gone out to him as it once had to Onar. Although she had still loved her older child, she had quickly become absorbed with the newborn. *Perhaps I started Onar's sourness. He was not always aloof. After Erlin's birth, he brought me—almost shyly—a baby bird for Erlin to play with; he danced in front of me and sat propped against my legs listening to me tell of the garden.* But each of these mental images, instead of soothing her, was painful, for little Onar's loving manner in those moments—though frequently spoiled by his attacks on Erlin—made her feel all the more guilty.

CHAPTER EIGHT

 THE snake was gray like the silt of a dry stream bed. It slithered on the rocks below Risha, who stood alert, unmoving, holding a stout club. Risha's eyes followed every motion of its body. She watched the serpent move inch by flowing inch on the slate-colored rocks and dust, camouflaged except for its sinister movements. She carefully let the club slide to the ground as she crouched, still staring at her enemy, and then in both hands lifted a flat slab of rock as long and thick as her arm. The serpent continued moving toward the sun-baked stones, seeking a place to nap under the hot sun.

Good, she thought, as it started coiling a short distance to her right. *Coiled in a nice, tight ring, it makes a much more satisfactory target.* As she lifted higher the heavy, sharp-edged slab of black rock, she looked to each side. Other snakes, she knew, might emerge from these rocks, with fangs behind darting, red-forked tongues. She shuddered; then she lifted her weapon above her shoulders, angry as she always was at this moment, thankful she had found a rock of such weight. She heaved it in a shallow arc, and stifled a scream as it missed his head and the center of the fat, coiled body but smashed into a section near its tail. Silently, her fingers scrabbled for a grip on the corners of the second rock slab she had chosen. *Another half second,* she thought.

But then she saw it was trapped, wriggling to free itself. Risha stopped her second throw in mid-motion. If the snake was trapped, she could take time to aim with more care. She forced herself to wait until it finally stopped its panicked writhing and lay momentarily still. She paused, aimed for its center, and heaved. The boulder crashed into the snake dead center and she enjoyed the sight of the terrible snap of its head.

Risha stood watching the creature in its death throes. It might take hours, she knew, for it to die. Once she had pinned a large copperhead and had left it. When she had returned a half day later she found a sight which had both sickened and satisfied her. An enormous black snake had started to engorge the trapped, poisonous one, and had ingested about a third of it. She had stood before that sight like a bird before a cobra, nauseated and entranced. She had taken another large rock and dropped it on them. "May you both be food for the vultures and worms," she had said aloud. But her rock had hit only the dead snake, and the feeding black snake had disgorged its meal with remarkable speed and shot away before she had been able to raise another boulder.

Although this ledge and rock plateau were far from their cave, she came here often; it was perfect for stalking snakes. She had learned the best times to catch them sunning. There was something about being on the hunt for her enemies which gave her a sense of purpose.

But Kael ridiculed her passion. *Kael, who nearly died from the loathsome beast. I suffered more that day than he,* she thought as she walked home. *The snake dropped on his neck, and it was I who saw those fangs strike Kael's flesh. Then came those days of his shaking and sweating with the poison, while I lived with the fear of being left alone. Kael felt none of that, lying asleep while his body battled the serpent's juice and I battled it with my tears and prayers and wet cloths to his body. I pleaded with Aaael for his life.*

She stood now before the cave, peering at her mate crouched within. As she had expected, Kael looked up from his task of skinning a marsh deer but did not greet her. She resented his disapproval, the firm set of his jaw as he methodically peeled the skin from just above the animal's black, divided hoof.

"Where is Erlin?" Risha asked.

"Tending the new lambs. He's *working*."

"Working?" The accusation in his tone angered her. "Who was up before dawn, bringing the wood for the fire? Who labored in the field jabbing holes for the grain?"

"Enough!"

Risha despised the authoritative manner her mate used with her. It accused her of being unworthy, of being the cause of all his troubles.

"So you drag yourself off to kill snakes," Kael said. "For what purpose? You refuse to eat them, although that might improve your disposition."

She winced. Usually Kael did not make sarcastic comments; his attack caught her off guard, and she sat down heavily on the soft foxtail barley that made up her bed.

"My disposition," she said, "is not aided by your wit. I suppose, though, *you* could eat snakes—you're cold enough. Poisonous, at times, too."

"You made the snake that way!" Kael accused.

"Intolerable!" she exclaimed. "It tempted *me!* It seduced *me!*"

"So you've said," he replied coldly.

"Even Aaael knew *that* was true! You saw him curse the serpent! You cannot think for a moment I originated—!"

"Perhaps," he said, interrupting her. "But if you hate the snake so intensely, shouldn't I hate you the same way?"

"Yes!" she screamed at him, even though she felt a terrible chill throughout her body. "Yes! Smash me with stones! They will hurt less than your holy judgments. You're like a bird pecking at my eyes. I came from you; how much did you warn and protect me? You and I did exactly the same: we listened; we ate, we disobeyed."

"But you did more," Kael insisted. "You dragged me with you."

"I can't stand this. Every night your dark, rigid face accuses me.

We lost the glory *together!* We're damned *together!*"

Their boiling emotions had taken both of them by surprise. Kael, she thought, seemed to have become immobilized and sat stiffly, his eyes intense upon her. Finally he resumed his skinning.

She watched him work. *Slowly, slowly, let the anger subside,* she told herself. The methodical movement of his knife held her eyes and calmed her. But she did not wish to take back her words.

She bit into a small plum and chewed as she began rinsing utensils. For about an hour they worked on various tasks, together and yet apart, each mind traveling in different paths. Once she tenderly touched him on the shoulder, but he did not respond.

"Kael," she at last said, softly. "I don't want to hurt you. Don't hate me."

He was cutting the deer's flesh into small strips for drying, and although he looked at her, he did not answer. Shortly thereafter, he finished his task and walked stone-faced into the wind outside.

Risha was left alone with her work. She noticed a silverfish on a wide rock at the entrance and walked over to squash it. She hated the dampness of the cave which allowed these things to breed. For a moment she watched it, like a thick, white-bellied eyelash gleaming on the rock, moving forward, exposed, naked under the sun. She moved. It stopped. She watched and eventually it shivered forward again. *I have the power of death over it,* she thought. *Not life, only death. It's like me, bewildered under the hot sun, out of its element.* She watched it crawl into a crevice. She dislodged a small rock, exposing it in its hiding place. The small rock rested in her hand, and suddenly she smashed the tiny thing. All that remained was a slight smudge.

Risha went back to her work, worrying about Kael's reactions. Later Erlin entered the cave; she hastily stood and greeted him. He nodded and she motioned toward the pot, about to offer him food, when he announced, "Father has selected a lamb for a sin offering. He's indicated you're to join him at the stones."

The sin offering! What was Kael trying to say? Instead of his usually affectionate manner, Erlin had about him an air of ritual formalism as he invited his mother to walk with him toward the stones.

She resented Kael's exclusive claim on the ritual. Aaael's voice had come to him in the bleak winter before Onar's birth, and it had been he alone who had gone to the mountain. He had returned full of instructions from Aaael to slaughter animals to atone for sin, all couched in bizarre descriptions of voices and flames and blood. But somehow through these things Kael had a certain hope and even peace.

They walked stiffly, awkwardly, over the familiar terrain until they reached a patch of smooth stones, which seemed like a white carpet for the trees. Onar stood upon the stones, his skillful fingers sharpening a branch with his knife, perhaps for use as a post, Risha thought vaguely. Kael was not in this little protected grove but evidently had instructed his sons to wait there. Risha saw him up on the ridge a long stone's throw from them. He had carefully shaped an altar out of large rocks. He was kneeling, spots of blood on his legs, his hands red with it, cutting and placing pieces of the butchered lamb upon the altar. Risha stood with Erlin and Onar, silent and motionless except for Onar's knife which impudently sliced against the wood and spread the slivers upon the stones at his feet.

Risha kept her eyes on her mate, who was skillfully completing his task. He worked at an angle from them; she could see the profile of his face and hands. She resented him, yet she also longed for him. She despised her needs, for she seemed as tied to him as to her own flesh.

What would he do up there, kneeling before that altar?

Kael stood now, tall against the darkening sky, and Risha thought of the days when she exulted in the prowess of his body. He stood looking into the distance, not moving. For perhaps a half hour he stood, the others watching.

Finally Kael sank to his knees. Risha could see that his face was con-

torted. He was grief-stricken, crying out to Aaael, but she couldn't catch his words. She stood kneading her knuckles together, and then reached out to Erlin, who did not object as their fingers intertwined. An insect crawled up her arm, but she ignored it. A sheep was bleating in the distance, annoyed at something. A dog yapped. But she heard

84

the sounds only faintly as she stared at her mate. *How can he humiliate himself in front of us?* she wondered.

It was already dusk when it happened. A great flame exploded into, or from within, the altar. Alarmed, Risha dropped flat on the earth at the loud *whoosh!* For an instant, she thought Kael was caught in it. But then she saw that he was moving back from the altar as the flames grew. *By now they've consumed all that was on the altar,* she thought, but still the flames rose, never wider than the altar, but ever higher. They whirled about like a windstorm.

Kael lay halfway between his family and the stunning energy of the flames. He remained prostrate. The flames shot higher and higher; they could see the tip continue to climb into the heavens, like a flaming star whose tail curled at their feet.

The flames continued to climb, now brilliant against the blackness of the night. All four lay flat upon the ground in that holy place.

Later, Risha found herself wakening in the sunlight, her sons beside her asleep, but Kael and the flames gone. How many hours had they watched? How many had they slept? Perhaps a day had passed by, for she was very hungry. Yet, her hunger for knowing Kael's fate was even greater.

CHAPTER NINE

 RISHA'S bare knees ground into the rocky soil as she labored along the rows of herbs, pulling green, sometimes prickly weeds. She kept a small garden of cooking herbs and spice roots, and now she pressed herself to complete the job before the sun was at its height. Already sweat had trickled into her eyes and dirt smeared her face where she had tried to clear her vision. She hated this work.

Yet she needed a methodical task to relieve her anxious thoughts. Kael was still gone. Had he been taken up in the flames, perhaps, while she slept? She had looked everywhere. Had she once again been rejected? Her fear of Kael's experience at the altar mixed incongruously with her desire for him. She longed for release from her bitterness. Yet she clung to it also, as her only defense, her only handhold.

Then she saw Kael's legs a few feet from her. Silently the man had come; she wondered how long he had been there watching. *On my knees before him,* she thought ruefully. *How fitting.* Yet she swallowed down that voice of self-pity and kept working to finish the task. At the end of the little plot, she tossed the last handful of weeds into the woods, then stood stiffly, trying to get her balance after being on her knees for so long.

She sat down on a fallen tree and greeted her mate cautiously. As she looked into his face, her fears increased. Kael's eyes had a brightness she had not seen since their expulsion. In fact, even in the garden his eyes had not shown this burning intensity which startled and confused her. How was she to deal with such strength?

"I have wounded Aaael," he said. "I have sinned against him."

His words were oddly contradictory to his expression, Risha thought. He was admitting guilt, yet he looked peaceful.

"I've sought bitterness," Kael continued, "and it's spilled on you. I've hated you, even though you're my own flesh. All these years, I've deceived myself, thinking I was pleasing Aaael. I've refused to forgive you; I've ground you underfoot as if all the guilt were yours."

He spoke with ferocity, with assurance, with the air of a man who has seen a vision. And these words, so new and desirable, had a strange effect on her. She knew them to be true. Yet she also knew her own guilt. He stood in such a triumphant manner, confessing his past faults, that she saw herself not only equally guilty but utterly unworthy. His guilt seemed all of the past but hers of the present. She was amazed that he would confess his wrongs against her. She wanted to respond in a way that would give them both joy, but she did not know how, for she resented his having gone before her into peace. She longed for the days of their innocence, when they spoke freely and intimately. Now, he spoke to her from his new vision, but she felt that she sat before a pillar of fire. He was victorious. She felt consumed by her own selfishness. He had wrestled with the gods—or with Aaael himself—and somehow had won, while she had been flattened before that consuming fire and was unchanged. She groaned inwardly, but her face betrayed no emotion.

"I have thrust the old ways from me," Kael said.

It was obvious he was not bragging but explaining his new resolve. Yet here was lost the great chance for their souls to meet. His next words, though meant to draw her up, drove her still lower. "And you, too, Risha, must renounce your rebellion. Peace lies at the heart, ready to rush in. Like dammed water released! You, too—" and he spoke on, but while describing all she ultimately desired, he fanned her resentment. He was too clean and victorious for her simply to say,

"Yes, yes, I will renounce," for she felt no compunction toward Aaael nor holiness nor light. She hated Kael, she hated herself, and she desired to see the hatred in Kael's face which he had had before his experience at the altar, that she might lash out against it. But there was none.

He grasped her cheeks in his two hands and raised her face to his. Then he kissed her lightly on the lips and turned away.

She often wondered after that what would have happened if he had kissed her hard on the lips and wept with her. Would she have wept with him? But in a strange way his mood would not allow more conversation.

A bird was insulting some creature nearby and its shrill chatter invaded Risha's thoughts. She continued sitting for a time, idly rubbing two stones together, grinding the dirt between them. She resolved to stand, to act, not to morbidly relive these events again and again. She called on her body to push, pull, stretch, work through her regular chores.

Her feet moved under her toward the deep stream nearby. She removed her clothing and bathed, luxuriating in the cool, rushing current. She splashed water into her face and rubbed her knees with her hands, then soaked under the hot sun, wanting the water to wash away not only the dirt in her pores but also her feeling of numbed indecision.

She rose physically refreshed and walked toward their cave. There she found a large basket she had woven from marsh leaves. After a long time of gathering berries and fruit, her basket was so full she had to hang the clusters of grapes on the side. With a small pot newly filled with creek water, she began a trek to the upper hills where she knew Erlin would be with his herd. He'd be glad for cold water and fresh fruit after his meal of meat and roots, and she would be refreshed by his voice and, she hoped, his laughter and his touch.

Erlin was higher up than she had anticipated, but she found the walk

soothing and invigorating, although she began feeling sweaty again. Her son was sitting on a thick tree limb, rocking back and forth slowly. She stopped and watched him. Every few moments his lips would move as if he were speaking, and twice she thought she saw him smile, but it might have been an expression he was using in his imagined conversation. He seemed thoroughly content there, the wind blowing his hair back. How different this long, muscular boy was from the child who had come running at her call and leaped into her arms. Now, Erlin could lift her easily, and his mind was complex and subtle. Month by month, she had felt him slipping from her, from the closeness which had nourished and sustained her.

"Erlin," she finally announced after a very long time of watching him, "I have brought you a snack and some cold water."

Her son opened his eyes, greeted her, and dropped easily out of the tree. He led her to a little knoll in the shade where they sat and, after he had taken a long drink, began eating.

The last time they had sat under a tree was at the altar, and although he smiled and laughed several times at her attempts at levity, he seemed still to have the vision of the ascending flames before his eyes. *As I do,* Risha thought.

90

"Mother," Erlin was saying, "what happened at the sacrifice? Have you forgiven Father?"

His question startled her. She paused, and for a bewildered moment simply stared at him. Finally she replied, "Forgiven? Who am *I* to forgive? He has received the forgiveness of Aaael; why does he need any of mine?"

"Mother, you know he wants your blessing," Erlin said rather formally, obviously risking his relationship with her. "He's been broken before the Powers, and you'd both be healed if—"

"Erlin! How am I to heal him? I am the one judged and guilty; I am the one who bears—"

"No! You both bear it! But he has reached out to Aaael and to you. Will you accept him as Aaael has?"

Risha was confused. Her son had never thrown such personal, penetrating questions at her before. Even though his tone was kind, his words wounded her.

"Of course I will," she said quietly, almost in a whisper. "I never saw it as a question of my forgiving him. He has not yet forgiven me—"

"What do you think he was saying to you?" Erlin asked sharply. "He can't say it well, perhaps, but he longs for you to know Aaael as he—"

"He told you he would speak to me?" she asked. The fear of an alliance of Erlin and Kael against her struck the depths of her security. Were they discussing her? Was she the "problem" which her beloved Erlin and husband had to solve? A fresh wave of resentment and even embarrassment flushed her cheeks.

"You are my very soul, Mother. I know well all of Father's many faults. I'm only saying that he has done all he can and now it's your turn to make peace with him and with Aaael."

"Oh, that I could! That I could!" she exclaimed. "But they've always accused me without mercy. Haven't I confessed again and again?"

"Yes, you have. But have you also confessed your resentments?"

How could a boy—a man perhaps, but barely—how could a boy, and she would ever call him that, see so clearly into her heart? "I'll think about what you're saying," she responded, realizing she had to give him some small victory if she were not to promote his alliance with Kael. She led the conversation into trite comments. Then she left, smiling weakly, promising again to consider his words. Yet she wanted with all her soul to lash out at his attack on her.

She walked with the nearly empty basket of fruit on her arm. Work. What task could she apply herself to now, that she wouldn't morbidly sit and stare? Her security of twenty years love between Erlin and her had been breached. The world shuddered and cracked under her: how was she to contend with this? How much truth was in his words? She needed to be doing something to clear her mind, but she did not want to be in the cave nor garden lest Kael should break into her thoughts.

She would search for food in the forest, she decided. She had the basket already in her hand, and she would see what she might find there, and perhaps explore beyond her normal bounds. She strode toward the trees, which rose hundreds of feet before her, and entered the cool interior. She loved the cavern-like openness and privacy of the forest.

As she walked, birds and small animals scurried in the thick layers of leaves and needles. She allowed the events of the last day to wash through her, not trying to arrive at any conclusions. Her eyes mechanically searched for food, and her feet conveyed her body across the crunching leaves. Her conflicting desires teased at her like dogs yanking at garments with their teeth, shaking them first this way and then that. Once she saw a rabbit scurry away. Startled, she called out to it, but it didn't stop, and she watched its white tail bounce into the distance. She wanted to reach out and stroke its back, but she could no more do that than unrestrainedly embrace Kael.

The words of her son pricked her. Once again she was the guilty one; yet this reflexive self-pity did not satisfy her as before. She noticed several large orange mushrooms with purple spots and sat down heavily among them. She picked one and marveled at the ribbed construction of its stem, the moist flesh which collapsed at her finger's pressure, the sturdy, spotted roof. She picked up one, then another, tossing them into her basket, thinking: *beauty even here, but we nearly died learning which beauty could kill us.* She leaned back against a tree with thick slabs of bark. She ripped one off, with considerable effort, to make a comfortable backrest and then settled herself against the tree.

As she sat with light sifting through the trees and a bird singing in the distance, she heard a voice high above her. She thought she had perhaps drifted into sleep and was dreaming. But the voice came louder, and it startled her from her drowsiness. She looked up, up the full height of the tree against which she had been leaning, and saw, distorted at that distance in the bright, filtering light, the figure of a man.

She was astounded. How could Kael have found her here? Why would he have followed her? Why would he be at the top of a tree? And why, equally peculiar, would he be greeting her in such a merry voice?

The figure began descending rapidly from the great height, calling out happy comments about the airiness of the day and the light uniquely bathing the forest like a golden mist. Risha saw that it was not Kael. Yet how could another man be in her world? She looked at the descending figure as if he were a tree come to life.

CHAPTER TEN

RISHA wondered if this man might be some celestial creature of an entirely different order from herself. His descending form seemed part of the diffused sunlight among the leaves. Yet as the man drew closer, she saw that he had flesh like hers. He was very tall, thicker framed, lighter skinned.

"You mistook me for someone else. I could tell by your expression," the stranger said, greeting her. He peered down jauntily from the branch above.

"Then your eyes must be more penetrating than mine!" Risha said. "I couldn't even see your face up there."

"Ah," the man remarked easily, almost nonchalantly as he leaned against the tree and cracked a nut between his thumb and forefinger, "I do see well." He was smiling with such an engaging boyishness that she felt drawn to him. She wondered why, though she had never seen this person before, she was instantly at ease with him. "Why are you sitting here alone in the forest?" the man asked.

Risha did not want to discuss her situation. "Perhaps for the same reason you were sitting at the top of a tree. Were you looking for the sun up there?"

"Of course!" he said. "Found it, too. From there you can reach up and pull out its fiery snow, and if you eat it, the stuff is cold on your tongue."

Her mouth dropped in mock exasperation. She was standing opposite him, leaning against a thick acacia, imitating his stance and trying to adopt his easy humor.

"Do you live in the forest?"

"Of course," he replied immediately.

"And what do you do here?"

In response he reached into the neatly cut skins which formed a covering over his loins and drew out a hollow stick about the length of his hand. He put it to his lips and blew, and a merry music sailed into the glade. As he blew, he also plucked strings which were somehow cut into the center of the instrument. The effect upon Risha was captivating, as if bubbles of music were entering her blood and floating with the air into her lungs. It drew her instantly into nostalgia for the songs she once sang in the garden. How long since she had sung to the delight of the animals!

She listened to him play skillfully, at first tapping her fingers against the ridges of the bark under her hand, then humming with the tune, and finally breaking out into song with him, singing of the sunshine and the forest and the colors of butterflies and mushrooms and tiny woods flowers and soft, thick needles under foot. She sang without the least embarassment, as if they had always sung together. It seemed to her all the forest creatures from birds to crickets were joining with them, although she realized it was her imagination.

Their music ranged from the silly, syncopated tappings about chipmunks and sparrows to majestic near shouts to the mountains and stars. When the man finally replaced the little instrument, her eyes were wet and her vocal cords sore. "Who taught you that?" she asked. "Were you also in a garden?"

If the man had said yes, her next question would have been, "Have you, too, incurred Aaael's wrath?" She wasn't sure what she wanted his answer to be, but he instead countered with "No, in a forest. And you have not yet told me what you are doing in my trees."

"I came to find you, of course," she said. "To hear your music. Do

96

you have a dwelling? Or do you live in the trees?"

"You may see for yourself. If you walk as energetically as you sing, we'll be there before I can learn your name."

"Risha," she said with a smile.

"I am Uilades." They questioned each other about their origins as they stepped through the forest. Both were evasive. Questions were answered with counter questions; Risha, by the time they were near his dwelling, realized she had learned very little about him, but she had revealed the basic facts of her life with Kael and her sons. She also realized that she had revealed many of her frustrations, though she had shared nothing of their expulsion by Aaael.

"Here we are," he said.

At first glance, she did not realize she was looking at Uilades' home. He had chosen trees for the basic structure, to which he had added logs which fit precisely into the surroundings. As she walked closer, she saw the logs and weavings of grasses formed a tight roof and walls. They had to stoop slightly to enter, and she feared it would be dark within. But it was not, for the sunlight easily found its way through the artful weavings.

The interior was simple, with only a few bowls and utensils stacked in a corner. She thought of the bower she and Kael had once shared. *"Rotted now, like dead flesh,"* she murmured, hating their damp cave. On the walls of Uilades' home were instruments of wood: hollow shapes with odd contraptions and holes; many strings stretched upon slabs of wood; circular bent branches. She reached out for one and handed it to him.

"Play!" she urged, and she sat on the leafy floor to listen. Between songs, he explained how he had gotten the idea for each instrument, how he had selected the wood, what he did to prepare the various types of strings.

How carefree this man seemed. How was he able to do it, alone here in the forest? Was he alone?

97

"Never," he told her. "I have the animals and birds. But I had no one to talk with, until you showed up at the base of my favorite tree. Which, of course, creates a very unusual bond between us."

"You're always jesting, aren't you? I'm not sure I like that." She felt a bit uncomfortable; their conversation seemed contrived. But she smiled, as if in apology. "I mean, you're more than light talk. You, too, have a face that has known pain. You *know*—more than that thrush and field mouse. How can you live alone?"

"I wasn't always alone," he said, adjusting with some seriousness. "Yes, I'm not a man-shaped mouse gamboling in the forest. But I'll be fair to you. Tell me all of your own story, for I'm sure it's far more interesting than mine, and then when you've told me everything, I'll withhold nothing about myself."

She stiffened a bit. "You sing and play the songs of Aaael. You live with the leaves and sun. You'll despise me when you hear my story."

"I could never despise you," the man said. "Your heart is too good."

"You're quite ignorant of my heart."

"Perhaps. But the question is, 'What made your heart become what it is?' You must tell me your story."

His manner was so engaging that she told him everything, the paradise in which she had once lived and what had happened because of the serpent. As she spoke, she kept blinking back the moisture in her eyes. Uilades lounged against a heap of rushes piled in a corner, one knee up, a small stick between his incisors which he chewed and twisted. His expressions kept changing to blend with her moods. He grunted in appreciation at the mention of songs and visitations and Kael's love, but winced sympathetically as she described the serpent's lies.

Risha found it difficult to tell him the whole story. Who was this man who played the joy songs of Aaael? Was he one of those pure ones who would judge her as all those heavenly powers had, even Shia? She hated to destroy their camaraderie. His face and manner were accepting, but what was he thinking as she told of the fruit between her teeth?

Uilades continued to murmur sympathetically, as if he had expected such a tale. When she told of their first attempt to find shelter after their expulsion, and of their clumsy attempts at hunting and trapping, he suddenly stood to his feet and exclaimed, "How monstrous! You were thrown into a living death!"

His words and expression were so empathetic they brought on her tears. Year after year after year she had longed to hear such words from someone who understood what she had endured. To hear this from such a solicitous friend broke down her composure, and she wept.

He came to her and very gently raised her to her feet and touched her wet face with his rough but gentle hands. He kissed her on the forehead as lightly as the touch of butterfly wings and then hugged her like a child, patting her softly and telling her, "This is good. This is very, very good, to speak of it, to share it, to get all those brackish waters out of your soul. Weep . . . for then you can laugh again." He continued caressing her shoulders paternally, and then told her to sit where he had been lounging, which she did obediently.

"But now," she demanded, trying to regain control of her voice and inject a bit of lightness to it, "we must hear your story."

"Yes. Very soon. I will tell it all. You'll be amazed and comforted by it! But I must know a few more things, for your story has touched me so that I cannot jump from one emotion to another. Tell me of Kael."

"Kael?" She started up a trifle and then leaned back, the self-pity rising to her throat again. "Why do you ask of Kael?" she said, trying to get more time to prepare her answer.

"Because he's half the story. What are you thinking right now?"

"Kael judges me harshly."

"He probably hates himself more than you, but he lashes out at you because—"

"No! He is pure and holy and reconciled; he calls down the Aaael-fire, but I am rejected! Rejected by him! Rejected by Aaael! Rejected by my own son! Only the bloody earth doesn't reject me; it will rot my flesh in its blanket!"

Risha felt ashamed at her outburst. She feared he would judge her harshly now. He was no fool, clearly. If she herself admitted that all her family—and Aaael himself—was judging her, wouldn't he conclude she was the guilty one? And perhaps he would be right, she thought, panicked.

He moved to her again, sat beside her and put his arm around her shoulders. "Not rejected by me," he insisted with his imperturbable, soothing tones. "Nor, perhaps, by anyone else. But even if they have —perhaps you see things more clearly than they—"

"More clearly than Aaael?"

"Of course not more clearly than Aaael, who sees all things as they are. But you may be assuming too harsh a judgment from him. You think he hasn't forgiven you? *You* haven't forgiven yourself. He is simply your teacher and maker. As for your boys, they're children. What can they comprehend? And if your tone says anything, your husband doesn't understand you. Perhaps he understands very little." He patted her arm, then gave her a little hug and moved away. "But Kael is not the point. Has Aaael treated you unjustly? Are you angry with him? If so, that's far more basic than Kael!"

"How can I be treated unjustly by Aaael when he *is* justice?" Risha asked, bitterness in her voice.

"Perhaps he just hasn't been paying attention lately," he responded wryly.

Risha looked up at him sharply and probed his eyes. "Do you jest?"

she asked, "or do you suggest that Aaael is like us?"

Uilades winked both eyes at her and smiled. "I jest, of course," he admitted. "I was trying to lift your mood a little. Risha, you take every little thing in life too seriously."

"Including Aaael?"

"Yes, of course including Aaael. We can displease him by caring too much. He didn't make us to wander about morosely, worried that he might dislike the way we get up in the morning. Aaael is the last one to want you in this bitter state."

Risha stood up and walked pensively to the entrance to the dwelling. "Do you speak of the Aaael of fire and blood and judgment? Do you know what Aaael wants? Tell me your story, so I can see what you know."

Uilades walked to her, put his arm protectively around her. "Let's take a walk," he said, "and when we step among my high aspens, I'll tell you anything you wish."

They started down a steep incline and he let her lead the way around some thick bushes. "Your body," he said, "moves as gracefully as the leopard. You grace my forest like the peacock. You must delight the eyes of Kael."

Risha did not know how to take such praise, for she was unaccustomed to it. She had ceased thinking of herself as beautiful.

A rivulet of water curved around a large oak with thick grass heaped up around its bole. He motioned for her to sit beside the water and dipped his fingers into the shallow flow. "Don't you see?" he asked, looking intently into her face, "can't you tell that beneath my songs and clever words there's sadness? I've lost something, too," he said cryptically. Uilades scooped water into his palm and held it up before her. "There's more death in my hand than life." He spoke as if accusing someone. He stood suddenly, flinging the droplets of water against the back of the oak.

"The wild!" he said, and she thought he expressed it as a man possessed, as intense as a snared bird watching an approaching hand. "All around us is death! A thousand fingerlings die for one to live, and then it dies anyway in a bird's beak. Everywhere flesh is wriggling, gasping, dying. All the world's fecundity feeds death. Have you felt the terror of a shrew in the mouth of a cat?

"But not you! Not you!" he suddenly insisted, touching her shoulders lightly. "You are the link to the other worlds. You are the seed for new beginnings. You are the object of Aaael's love and you took the risk and have suffered all. But through you, *through you* Aaael will put the world right again! It is promised!"

Risha was completely confused by this outburst. It was the first time Uilades seemed out of control. Yet his words kindled strange hope. His passion at the state they were in resonated precisely—remarkably—with her own indignation. She had risen to face him and his hands were again on her shoulders. He looked compassionately into her face as if she were suffering for him, as if he and all the universe were grateful, and as if he empathized with her anguish, yet worshiped her. All this she read in his expressions, and she was thrilled to have a companion who did not judge her, but stood with her.

They stood for several moments, silent. Then, "But you are not to take all this so seriously, Risha, as I have warned you before, and warned myself also." He impishly, impudently pushed his nose into her hair which hung by the sides of her face. He whispered into her ear, caressed her cheeks, teased and praised her, speeding her pulse. She responded with her hand on his as it moved gently on her skin. "You must wake up again to life!" he whispered. He hinted that she was made not only for beautiful clothing, but a better life and a regal pride. He rested his hands on her shoulders, then let them plane down her back and up again, massaging her back, interjecting slight parental pats.

"Your hair tumbles down your shoulders like rushing waters," he whispered. He seemed to know all she wanted to hear, and on every point he skillfully defended her against Kael. He never criticized Aaael, but again and again he pointed out that she played a heroic role in the affairs of the planet and must assert herself to please Aaael. He hinted that perhaps Aaael did enjoy her discomfort, but she must be strong. Uilades was a man who fully understood her, she thought, who cared in a way Kael never had, who desired her for what she was and might yet be. This man touched her with laughter and love.

She desired this man, but a thought about Erlin watching this scene suddenly introduced a tinge of shame. She looked up at Uilades. His expression perplexed her, for it seemed one of design, not passion. His eyes were distracted, as if he were contemplating something else. She thought of the way he had been touching her from the beginning, small, innocent gestures, which led to intimacies. Her sense of shame intensified. Were the movements of Uilades' hands a trifle mechanical? Was all this her imagination, or was she being seduced? What was she doing here with this man anyway? She did not even know who he was. In fact, he had still successfully avoided telling her anything of his "fascinating story." Anger began displacing passion. She realized with certainty that the man was lying. His praise for her body, she thought ruefully, spoke of her not as she was but as she had been. He ignored the birth creases on her belly from Erlin and the hard lines around her mouth and eyes. He was not interested in pleasure, but something else.

His mouth was on her naked shoulder, nibbling and kissing it. "Your lips are evil!" she screamed suddenly. "They are wriggling snakes upon my flesh!"

Her sudden movement caught him off guard. She saw again that his expression was indeed strangely detached. He caught himself, but not before she knew something possessed this creature of the forest. "Who are you anyway?" she demanded.

She sensed he was struggling to control himself, but she couldn't tell what his passions were. What was he? With a cry, she leaped from the rivulet and the nearness of his breath and raced away through the woods. A strange tearing noise came from his throat and she heard him calling out to her, his feet pounding mere paces behind. The sound of his feet nimbly crunching and leaping through the tangled underbrush made her run faster than she thought she could; terror controlled her legs.

Even so, he would surely be faster here in his own element, would know all the ways of cutting her off.

She made her way up a hill, trying to dodge the briars whipping against her legs. She was nearing the hill's crest now and saw that she was at the lip of what seemed a cracked half-bowl, the base of which was far below her where she saw sparkles from water. She crashed along the edge of the rocky, tree-lined ridge, the pursuer close behind.

She saw the break in the ridge quickly enough to make a decision. It was a long gap which, with effort, could be leaped. At its edge grew trees which she could grasp. It was either turn sharply and run downhill toward the water, or race straight for that rift and leap. As she ran, trying to pace her steps so she would have momentum for the jump, she wondered what good this would do her, since her pursuer could surely leap equally well. But as her body gracefully flew over that space and her fingers grabbed for the tree roots which would support her, she knew what she would do as soon as she scrambled up the other side. She searched for a stick—any sort of stick. She dared not look far, for she heard him only yards behind, dodging the same brambles, using the same rocks for footing, moving as fast as she. There! Lying in the leaves, a piece of half-rotted trunk about the thickness of her leg. She grabbed for it, twisting her whole body—one swift motion to face the pursuer. He was in the last seconds of his approach to leap as she did. In the same motion as her turning, she

saw she must stop him instantly, so she screeched at him, "No!" She repeated her cry as she gripped the supporting trees with her stick held out fiercely like a spear.

Uilades could barely change his forward motion and grabbed for the base of a thin ash to stop him. At the last instant he'd seen that the stick might cut short his leap just enough for his fingers to miss the trees on her side. Even if his fingers held, she could pound loose his handhold at the crucial moment of impact and he would be cast down.

Risha stared at his sweaty face. He lay twisted on the ground where he had sprawled. His face was contorted with muscle spasms he was obviously trying to control. He rubbed his forearm across his lips, licking the little blood droplets from the scratches. Risha had scarcely been aware of all the cuts in her own skin but glanced at her legs and saw red stripes criss-crossing her calves, oddly delicate designs on her sweaty muscles.

They stared at each other for long, long moments, regaining their breath, Risha still holding the stick. Uilades' eyes explored the chasm and the ridge that went from his feet to the right and around her. That route would take time, and by then, she might escape.

At last he spoke, though he still appeared full of strange emotions which might have been rage, or indignation—or even fear. Yes, fear, she thought, mixed strangely with rage. And a hunger, a predatory hunger. Her terror did not abate as he spoke soothingly, "Why are we doing this? One moment we are talking with great joy of having found each other, and then you run like an animal with a spear in its side. And I—I'm distressed at my clumsiness. I simply can't let you disappear." He talked on and on.

"I was frightened," she said at last. "Let me go home. I won't think harshly of you. Let me return, and another day, perhaps, we'll see each other again." It was dusk already and she was becoming extremely anxious that he leave before darkness took away her advantage.

106

He continued talking, trying to persuade her to let him come over and show her he meant no harm whatever. Had he done anything she had not encouraged? He was standing now, poised to leap, evidently hopeful that his arguments were having some effect. He pulled back a trifle, in position to spring forward, but as she saw his muscles tighten, she screamed at him with the same ferocity as before and held the stick so that it would thrust into his throat or chest. His reaction was strange; his face became white, as if the blood had drained entirely from it, yet his eyes bulged and his lips tightened; he glared at her with what was now evident hatred and hunger.

Then the greater horror began. At first it was a distortion of his face, as if the bones were being twisted and expanded from the inside. His eyes—was it her imagination?—began almost imperceptibly to separate from each other. No, it was not her imagination, the skin was stretched taut. Even his forehead seemed to be expanding and the skin tightening as Risha looked on with the stick tight in her hand.

Then the skin split between his eyes. Only a light trickle of blood appeared, but the split kept rising up his forehead even as the blood lightly edged down beside his nose and neared his distorted mouth. The expansion continued and finally his skull, impossibly distended, cracked open at the forehead. Instantly, a dark, oily protuberance poked its way out. Risha thought it beak-like, but it was shaped less like a beak than the sharpened point of a stick. The projection expanded and grew out of the living skull, with what seemed an eye right behind the sharp beak projection. The thing that expanded and split its way out of Uilades—the lifeless Uilades, whose dead hand still grasped the sapling—was impossible to describe precisely. The emerging horror growing larger and larger was dark and gray. She sensed a flapping of bat wings and the menace of snake fangs, yet she saw neither of these. *Never in Aaael's world!* she thought. *There's nothing in Aaael's world like this!* The thing tore free from the broken body of Uilades, which then collapsed. She screamed at the advancing thing. *"Fiend!* Have you stolen yet another body? Fiend! So that is you!" but she said it not in power or rage but revulsion and helplessness as it spread its dark, oil-gray wing-shapes and rose into the air above her, large, hideous, ill defined.

"Aaael!" she screamed aloud. "Aaael! Aaael!" She called on her only hope even as she brandished her puny stick.

The thing descended upon her as soon as she called out Aaael's name. She thought, because of its reaction, that perhaps her cries to Aaael might have meaning, so she called more loudly, "Aaael! Aaael!" as she struck out with her stick at the grotesque mass coming down upon her face.

The stick shuddered in her hand as it struck the thing attacking her, but it did not break. The impact, she thought, was like hitting wet sand which splatters apart. The apparent success of the blow encouraged her as she continued to scream Aaael's name into the darkening forest. She swung again at the horror, and again hit a cloying wetness which separated heavily with the impact. Was it her fevered mind, or had the stick, as she cried out to Aaael and struck with it, shriveled part of the odious mass? She struck at it again and again.

Suddenly she heard its departing cry of rage which she could never thereafter forget. It was a scream of unsated hunger and cataclysmic loss that rocked so through the forest and through her that it shook her to her knees, as the creature flapped away from her and into the valley and its darkening shadows.

Risha collapsed among the trees and stared across the chasm. She sat in shock. Then, slowly her eyes began to focus on Uilades' body. His face was now recognizable, but it looked as if he had fallen upon it from a great height.

She slowly closed her eyes, then turned away. That Uilades was dead was sure, but with what had he ever been alive? The serpent's life? Was Uilades a mere egg sucked dry? No, she thought, he was more like the egg of an ostrich she had found one day, with a near-mature fetus which had died and rotted within, and which she had opened, hoping for food, only to find putrefaction.

And now? She did not know where to go in this dark forest, but she turned her back on the body and began cautiously feeling her way past the trees, away from it.

CHAPTER ELEVEN

THE quarter moon shone pale yellow but bright, and Risha kept her eyes on it, her arms groping before her to ward off branches. Looking up through the tall trees with their shifting leaf shapes helped her little in guiding her feet. But Risha's soul longed for that crescent of light above. At times it would be obscured by a hanging branch, then break through first as splotches of brightness, then as the thin shape like a familiar slice of fruit hanging in the sky.

But how much comfort was a bit of light, inaccessible in the night sky? Darkness had just begun; the hours ahead would seem interminable, she knew, and why should she believe that the scaly horror which had hungered for her would let her rest? Would it not attack her irresistibly the moment she slumped to the ground and released her grip on the stick? What had that foul apparition been? Surely the loathsome creature which had come from Uilades could not have such intelligence and grace as Uilades himself. Were both Uilades and the serpent mere hosts for the evil usurper?

She suddenly realized that she would never again stalk and kill the snakes of her valley; this thing which had emerged and hungered for her had in distorted ways something of snakes and serpents and slugs and larvae but only as a rotted corpse resembles a living body. Snakes, living, feeding, propagating snakes with their graceful motions and darting tongues, were coils of purpose and even beauty—yes, beauty, she had to admit.

Would the being which hungered for her give up on its prey in the dark of a pathless forest? "O Aaael," she whispered, "Aaael, Aaael!"

She saw by the moonlight before her two large trees which came together at their base in a V. She climbed up between them and rested, her back against one and her feet against the other. One hand she kept tight on the stick, while the fingertips of her other hand probed the rib-like bark of the tree. She continued calling Aaael's name softly, pleading into the darkness. She had no path; she had no light; to go on would be futile. All she could do was rest, and call into the night.

In the darkness, she could think of little else but the thing which stalked. She fought sleep for hours, imagining one strange silhouette after another coming alive in the branches above her. Every time she heard rustling leaves and small noises, she tried to visualize familiar birds and animals. Yet her fears grew larger with each sound. *Alone in the forest,* she thought, *afraid of a cricket or a deermouse. It's always been this way since my humiliation.* She felt tears welling in her eyes as she considered her plight, and they almost obscured a speck of light, like a star lowered into the trees. She blinked and tried to separate the light from the stars. Was she simply seeing a star at an odd angle? It looked as if it was moving among the trees, for it would disappear and then reappear, always a little larger, as if it were heading for her.

Light. It had to be a light, she decided, moving in the forest. And surely light would mean the fires of Aaael and not that of decay and death, she thought, enormously relieved. But almost as quickly as this elation arose, she wondered if the evil were using light to trick her. She cowered lower into the cradle of the rough-skinned trees which held her and thought of the muskrats and beavers in traps which had heard her footsteps coming.

The light grew larger, but now it did not seem to be coming closer but moved in a line which would pass by her. As she watched, she did not know whether to call out or to remain silent. Silence. Silence. She would remain quiet and listen with all her senses, for she thought she heard some faint sound near the light. Yes, a sound, but as she listened, it seemed to grow. The more she listened the more clear it became that this was a voice. A voice calling. But so faintly it called! Was it the faintness of the voice, or her skill at listening? The voice almost seemed to be coming from a different dimension, as if she had to attune her deepest faculties to its sound.

Then she recognized the name the voice was calling. It was her own. "Risha. Risha," it called, with such an otherworldly mixture of compassion and holiness that it caused her both joy and fear. She raised her face to the light but lowered her body even further into the tree. The voice kept calling her, and she had no strength or will to respond. The voice simply washed into her, and she absorbed it like nourishment. *His voice; it's Aaael's voice,* she thought. The sound brought vividly to her mind his graceful motions and most of all, his face. How she remembered Aaael's lips calling her name in the garden—oh, how she had loved her name on his lips, and his face looking at her with approval. How she longed for that look now.

But the voice calling her was not the approving one she had heard so often in the garden. This voice was one of righteous love, calling to her, demanding everything and welcoming her in the same tone.

"Father! Maker! Aaael!" she called out. "Let me see your face!"

He continued to call to her, but she feared rushing out to him. Feared him. The light by now was receding into the forest, and she did not want to risk a plunge into that darkness, nor did she know what would be required of her if she reached him and fell at his feet and looked into his awesome face. She cringed at her own ambivalence and called again. "Father! Maker! Aaael! I must see your face!"

But the light did not stop moving, and the voice was growing fainter, although he continued calling her name and she could still hear it.

The light disappeared among the trees, reappeared, and eventually was gone. But she still heard the voice. So long as she called out to Aaael, she heard him calling her name. It was almost as if the voice had always been there and always would be, like the sky and the moon. It filled her with conflicting emotions, but the voice reassured her that she was not cast off to become prey for the evil specter.

RISHA awakened as first light broke into the forest. She viewed her surroundings, then rolled stiffly out of the tree; as she hit the ground on all fours, she found it difficult to stand after lying in a bent position all night. Each motion of her body recalled the hard, ribbed bark against her back.

Except for a yellow finch darting from tree to tree, she saw no woods creatures. But the sunlight filling the forest lifted her spirits. Whatever had happened last night, she had not succumbed to temptation. This time, whatever the stakes may have been, she had not failed. And Aaael had been in the forest—somehow, strangely, *with her,* calling her name. True, she had not run to him. But for the first time since the catastrophe, she was thinking, *My heart even feels warm toward him. I want to be near and with him. Haven't I at last pleased him?* Perhaps the absurdity of expulsion from his presence was over and this sordid episode of blood and death and barriers finally done with. Her sons had not eaten the fruit—was it not more than time to let them into the garden? Perhaps there was even a small shred of vindication for her now. She had suffered; she had not fallen deeper. And had not Uilades said that by her all would be restored?

She determined that she would go right to the heart of the matter by going back. Having overcome temptation gave her joyous hope. She turned her face toward the garden. She would present herself humbly as the chastened heir, the one who had suffered all and had not failed in this final test. Surely Aaael wouldn't strike her down; hadn't he called to her in the dark forest? Didn't he remain her only Father?

Not until the sun was nearly above her did she orient herself enough to know she was finding the way back to her origins. Eventually the forest gave way to open fields, which were sliced through by the familiar river, so wide she wondered if she could swim its width without having eaten. She was beginning to feel weakened from hunger, even though she had found a few small nuts.

She followed the river's edge as she had so many times years before, her anticipation growing so great her body was shaking slightly. Home again! For the first time it seemed possible *now,* not in some remote half-dream of the future. *Ah, if I had only resisted temptation the first time,* she thought. *Here I am nearing the waters and trees and animals and Aaael's creatures where all is well.* She saw in the distance, where the river curved to the left, conifers rising enormously toward the sky, her sentient friends. She could see a great bird flying among them, and longed to recognize it and call out to it. *Ah, my home, my home, surely the longing for my home won't be denied.* Wasn't it innocent and right? She walked along crying, her tears like soft summer rain.

Risha began seeing through her tears a waving light. She looked for its source but it was widely diffused. Then she heard a sound, and as the light began focusing before her, the sound became the voice of Shia. Risha's face and eyes became radiant. She turned toward the living light shimmering and flowing from among the bushes of the forest's edge, not able to restrain herself from rushing to Shia and embracing her.

Shia responded with joy, returning Risha's embrace, laughing with her, radiating light. But Risha sensed immediately a certain restraint. They touched and smiled but did not speak, the impact of the reunion after so many years nearly overwhelming Risha. "Come," Risha finally urged, "let's walk toward the garden together."

"No. Let's sit here by the fig tree and the sycamore. I've been given liberty to speak to you and answer your questions—"

"I want to be done with questions!" Risha interrupted, her heart sinking. "My mind is sick with them; I simply want to go with you to the garden and be Aaael's happy child again! I make no claims; let us go up and you can instruct me in all you wish. Why delay?" Wasn't Shia an omen that she might re-enter? Would there be a long discussion of everything first?

"You cannot enter the garden," Shia told her flatly.

Risha flushed, then heavily, wearily sank down to the soft grasses. She wanted to speak and even scream for Shia to say they would go together to the garden. But all she said was, "Can we never go back?"

"The garden is not the same; you are not the same. All is changed and ever will be," Shia said. "But there's still hope."

Hope? A word? Hope? I cannot go back, but there is hope? "Shia," she accused, "why do you taunt me?"

The light of Shia's body imperceptibly changed to a deeper shade of bronze. "Risha, I would never taunt you. There is hope. For some, there is no hope. You met such a person in the forest."

Risha looked at her sharply. "Who was it? Or who were *they?*"

"Evil," Shia responded simply.

"But who? Was Uilades evil? What was the thing which pursued me? Did he wish to devour me?"

"Yes. In every way. But now he can feed only on himself."

Risha blanched at the directness of Shia's explanation. "But why has it waited all these years?"

"They have always been sowing dissension among you. It's your own lusts and rebellion that respond. They've longed for you and watched for your weakest moment. They cannot destroy you unless you invite them to." Shia stated this indignantly, and Risha blushed.

116

"What saved me then? My own refusal to give in? As I swung at the evil thing I knew that no mere blow could—"

"Yes, of course Aaael reached out to you."

"But Shia!" Risha exclaimed, "if he could rescue me in the forest in such danger, why can't we re-enter the world we were made for? Riddles. It makes me ache!"

Shia leaned back against a large sycamore tree and her bronze light flowed up the trunk above her shoulder like golden water flowing uphill. She silently watched the mortal.

"It was of Aaael that you withstood temptation," Shia said. "It was of Aaael and through him." Then Shia sat silent again.

Risha, looking at Shia's face, understood that she had resisted the seduction because she had feared the results, not because she had loved Aaael. What had she to do at all with resisting temptation? she wondered. Had she not been a mere cipher, led to one belief about Uilades, and fleeing only after she had realized the truth?

Risha sat looking into the compassionate face of Shia. "Was there not even a stone's worth of resistance from me?" she asked weakly.

"The question doesn't matter," Shia said. "You are still favored of Aaael. He's always there, calling, listening. I've said there's hope. Always cling to this. Through your seed shall come salvation. We're always watching you. Aaael knows your every thought—"

Shia's voice continued instructing, but her last comment frightened Risha. Every thought? If Aaael were judging her every thought. . . .

"But if these terrible dangers lust after me," Risha began saying, wondering if Shia also knew her every thought, "why can't you build a wall around us? If there's hope, why not *now!* Why can't you keep out the loathsome specters!"

"Because *you* let them in!" Shia said. "You have lighted the fire. You must walk through it. Aaael cannot change, nor can the universe."

"If only Aaael had never made me!" Risha exclaimed.

Shia did not respond to this. "The herbs of your cure are obscene to Aaael," she said. "But maybe they'll heal you, Risha. You love your diseases! You don't know yourself!"

"But all this for a piece of fruit!" Risha said.

"No. Not for a piece of fruit. All of us must choose. Aaael—or the other. You made a choice. Would you have done better at another test?"

Risha dropped to the ground, sobbing. Was it all to mean rejection *again?* Couldn't she simply fall into Shia's arms and cry out her pain and return to the life she was created for? She wept for a long time. A seed of anger began growing in her. Aaael's promises of hope—yes, she wanted hope, but why taunt her? Why shove her back to the dark forests and bloody valley? She was ready to come back to *him;* why couldn't he welcome *her?* But as she opened her wet eyes and lifted her face to say this, she saw that Shia was gone.

RISHA forced her feet the last few steps out of the darkness into the firelight. Kael sat with his back against the wall, his legs straight out and pointed at the fire, his hands mending a trap. Erlin was leaning back on his elbows with his knees up, staring at the fire. Onar sat on his haunches, breaking twigs between his fingers. She appeared among them suddenly, gaunt-faced with burning eyes, and although they quickly looked up, her embattled expression and tightly compressed mouth warned them to keep their silence. Her only words were, "I am not dead. Let me simply eat and sleep." The shadows moved about their faces as she stared at them, fighting her exhaustion, reaching stiffly for the cold smoked meat in a woven basket. She grasped the bone of a duck leg securely in her hand and chewed with determination, explaining nothing.

Her hunger the past day had goaded her resentful thoughts. Contrasted with the other events, hunger was a small hardship, but its unnecessary presence galled her. Shia had revealed that she was being watched, that the Aaael powers were ever about. Even as she trudged back in defeat with her empty, protesting belly, they watched. *Ah, how they love me,* she thought ruefully, *watching my every painful step, allowing me to be sport for their amusement. Couldn't Shia have at least fed*

me before deserting me? Shia, with all her mystical advice, exiles me, sends me back in humiliation.

She felt she'd accomplished nothing. Somehow she had failed to respond to Shia correctly. Failed. Failed. Failed. During the full day it had taken her to return through the fields and forest, the seeds planted by Uilades and nourished by her own resentments had grown. They had become a bittersweet pleasure. Her anger at being deserted by Shia had been reflexive and momentary, but this other thought was hardening within her. How could Aaael be good, if at the moment of her temptation, he had not intervened? Were all the higher powers evil? Or a mixture of evil and good? Wasn't she even now being tortured by the supposedly *good* powers?

As she sat at the fire gnawing greedily at the dark flesh of the fowl, keeping her gaze from the faces of her men, she could not dismiss the questions. *Why didn't Aaael rescue me when I was tempted the first time? I was a baby; an innocent. Would I leave my baby before a wolf and watch as the animal slowly stalked, creeping closer and closer? Would I watch—simply watch—as the wolf entranced my child, as its jaws reached for my child's throat? Would I sit silent as the teeth ripped the flesh and loosed the blood and then criticize my child for his judgment? Would I mutter, "I warned you, foolish child, about the fangs of the wolf. Sinful child, you became entranced with the wolf's soft coat and hypnotic motions; you must pay the gruesome price."* "Pah!" she muttered contemptuously, cracking the stripped duck bone to suck out the marrow. *Would I watch my child die? If I had warned him, "In the day you smile at the wolf, you die," would I be righteous in merely watching? Aaael watched me listen, and stumble, and fall. As the fangs of the serpent's words hit my throat, Aaael moralized about my desire for his fruit!*

Could Aaael be evil in a complex, subtle way? Did he sadistically use his creatures? *All I know is my own experience,* she thought, *and so far, my experience has amounted to hopes crushed and being stalked in the night.*

120

CHAPTER TWELVE

"WHAT have you been working on so intently?" Risha asked her younger son. "Not many projects could keep you from your midday meal." She handed him several small cakes with currants on top. Erlin took them from her and popped one whole into his mouth.

"I'm making a little pen for Troia to have her kid," he said. Troia was his favorite goat, russet brown with black and white markings. According to Erlin's calculations, she would give birth in two weeks. "But she refuses to wait until I'm done! Three times I've had to pick her up and carry her out of the pen. Even now I had to put up a barricade of logs to keep her out." He spoke affectionately of Troia, obviously amused at her desire to be in the pen.

Both ate the cakes hungrily and in between sampled some of the small blue grapes Risha had picked. Their skins were sour, but alternated with the cakes, they tasted good. Erlin ate hurriedly and after his eighth cake rose quickly from the hard floor.

Risha smiled at him. "Go and finish your project. I think your goat is getting a better bed from you than you have yourself."

It seemed to Risha Erlin had just left when he came rushing back to her. "It's born!" he announced. "She crashed through the barricade and got into that pen, and it's born! You've never seen such a lovely little creature. Come!" He was off, running back to his discovery before his mother could rise.

Risha had not seen Erlin so excited since he was five. She was grateful to share this experience for the bonds it would build with him. When she arrived, her son was already in the pen with the mother goat, reassuring it and patting its head. "Can you believe the persistence of this animal?" he asked his mother. "Troia knew. She probably wondered why I was so thickheaded as to think the birth must come later." He was thoroughly delighted, and as Risha looked at the newborn kid, she shared his excitement. Amazing, she thought, that something only moments old could look so steady on its thin stalks of legs. It was a light brown color that Risha found very pleasing, a color that drew her hands to pet and rub its still-wet hair. His belly was white, and his face perfectly marked, with black streaks along the sides of his face, and a white mark like a shaft of light from his forehead to his nose.

"What will you name him?" Risha asked.

"Koko," Erlin replied. "He is just the color of the cocoa fruit when it is dried and mixed."

"Precisely!" Risha agreed. "The color is so lovely it makes me want to use him for a pillow," and she put her cheek against his side. "A baby goat is never quite as soft—as indescribably soft—as a lamb just born. I can hardly keep my hands off a newborn lamb," she said. "But Koko seems soft yet muscled and graceful and ready to run so soon after birth. What a marvel!"

Erlin spoke in similar ecstatic terms about the new addition to his herd, and his boyish enthusiasm put Risha into a good mood for the rest of that day. Several times she revisited the pen and motioned to Erlin, who was busy in the meadow, to come over and join her, which he did gladly. She could almost believe, in all the fecund bursting of springtime, that life was normal and natural.

IN the years since her encounter with Uilades and then with Shia at the edge of the garden, Risha had come to an uneasy truce with Kael and the inner forces which tormented her. She envied and respected Kael's obdurate faith, yet despaired of it as well. At times she would long to participate in his rituals; at other times she would resent being pressured toward them. But what helped most in keeping her at peace with her family were moments like these with the newborn goat. With the snow and ice of winter and the flies and heat of summer came also the small joys of life: the exhilaration of a booming, flashing thunderstorm; her making first tracks in the season's first snow; baby snowshoe rabbits orphaned and snuggled in their cave. Risha tried to focus her life on such moments, and on the work, avoiding confrontations about the forces of Aaael which generated such chaos in her.

But for Kael, the sacrifice to Aaael was holy ritual, and he continually instructed his sons in its purpose. Risha was sufficiently awed to participate quietly.

A half year after Koko was born, however, came a new crisis. She saw Erlin leading the young goat to the hillock where sacrifices were made. Startled, she called out to him and strode to his side. "Where are you going with your favorite animal?"

"Only the best is good enough for Aaael," her son said shyly. She saw in his face how painful this was to him.

"You're to take fine animals from your herd, but you don't have to slaughter one that's become almost part of the family! Doesn't Koko follow you, rest when you rest, and run where you run?"

Erlin looked ashamed, yet at the same time resolute. "That's true, Mother," he said. "That's the point. The sacrifice is gravely serious.

123

My disobedience to Aaael is terrible enough to require my own blood. Koko is merely a substitute. You've heard this from Aaael more often than I."

"What you say is true," Risha said, feigning agreement, "but do you recall the time you were out playing with him, and you wrestled him to the ground?" She smiled infectiously, and he returned her smile, shaking his head in assent. "Then you got down on your knees —he was only a couple of months old, and always butting things— and you squared off with him. He came at you as if you were another he-goat, and you lowered your head and crashed right into his. Little Koko knocked you flat!"

Erlin laughed and rubbed his head, remembering the incident. "He was so small, I had no idea his head could be so hard! I went down as if a tree had fallen on me." Risha encouraged him to remember other incidents with Koko, and they talked affectionately of the little beast for a few moments as it impatiently pawed the ground with its small, black hooves, eager to scamper into the meadow. Then the stories ran out, and they shared an awkward silence. Without speaking, Erlin turned and started walking slowly—reluctantly, she believed, as she watched his shoulders—toward the hillock with the kid, a sharp blade in his hand.

Risha turned from the sight which so troubled her and resolved to

124

confront Kael. She ran along the rocky ridge which led to the lower fields where she hoped he would still be laboring, stopping just long enough to fill a jar with water for him. His form, bent low digging out potatoes, was visible as soon as she came to the end of the ridge. She knew that so long as Kael was here, there would be no ritual of sacrifice on the hill.

Hearing her approach, he forced himself up and pushed his back forward, sighing at the ache, but stretching pleasurably. His muscular body, dark under the sun and naked to the waist, pleased her and she playfully dipped her fingers into the cold water and splashed it on his sweaty shoulders and chest. He smiled at her and took the jar in his hands. As he drank the water in one long draught, she felt affection for him. Yet it mixed with her anger at Kael's encouraging Erlin to sacrifice Koko.

She never shared her conflicts with Kael, for he grew ever stronger in his belief, while she grew ever more tentative. She had never told him what had happened in the forest with Uilades, even though she longed to, for she felt she had gained a victory of some sort. Yet she was bewildered by Shia's rejection, and she didn't want to share that with Kael. She feared he would probe and probe and then pronounce judgment, that he would drag her out to prostrate herself before the altar and kill an animal and cry for Aaael's forgiveness, and hadn't she already done that in the forest? All she had ever shared with Kael about those days away from him had been Aaael's calling her in the darkness and her answering. She had done this in off-handed comments, to keep him from asking questions and also to establish her own private link with Aaael, to give her a little power against Kael's absolute spiritual authority.

"The water's still cold," he said in appreciation. "What brings you here?"

"I want you to help Erlin. But I also want to spend a few moments with you; we don't talk very often." He looked at her suspiciously, though he threw his sweaty arm around her as they walked to the shade.

They talked for a few moments, and even jested a bit about their intimacies, and then Risha said as they lay on their backs, looking at white and grey clouds, like distant mountains against the blue, "Erlin wants to sacrifice Koko. I don't like it, Kael. It's not natural. Koko is like a *person* to Erlin; it's a terrible thing for him to do this. He'll regret it. He'll lie at night thinking, 'What is Aaael that he demands I kill what I love?' "

"But he has talked to Aaael," Kael said. "He knows the price. Forgiveness and Aaael-joy—"

"But Aaael does not require *this* sacrifice."

"Erlin has called out to Aaael that he will do anything to atone for his sin—*anything!* This is what he believes Aaael—"

"Believes! How can he know? What does this child know of *sin?* How has he sinned? You don't want your son to morbidly pursue a false image of Aaael. I know how one can, in the night, become convinced of something, but realize in the morning—"

"Risha," Kael said rather sharply, "we have spoken enough. Erlin waits for us, and we can't delay what Aaael has ordained."

His curt, decisive statement jolted Risha, though she had experi-

126

enced such endings to conversations in the past. "You dismiss me like a dog that has rolled itself in carrion," she protested.

He refused to respond but stared coldly at her. "You make me feel repulsive," she shouted.

He continued to use his silence on her, and only after several moments pronounced, "Perhaps at times you are," then turned away.

She was enraged. How could this fellow being, this lover, Kael her husband, abandon himself in racking sobs to Aaael and be received by him in flames which fled to the stars . . . yet reject her? Risha followed him, full of resentment and no tenderness whatever, to take part in the ritual slaying of Erlin's pet. *Why must every good thing turn to blood?* she murmured. During the sacrifice, she talked to Aaael and almost asked him to intervene, but she feared even thinking this way . . . *Every time I reach out to Kael, or to Aaael himself, I am rebuked.*

Later, cracking nuts between stones in the cave, she wondered what kind of world she was in, that her son had to take what he loved most and kill it? She cracked the nuts vehemently, and a corner of the rock cut her thumb. She looked down at it dully, sucked it dry, and went on smashing the nuts.

CHAPTER THIRTEEN

 RISHA'S morning began with her usual routine: drawing water to fill two pots and carrying them into the coolness of the cave, washing in the refreshing stream water, attacking this day's major task: winnowing grains. Erlin had eaten breakfast with them, and she did not think it unusual when he did not return for his noon meal; he would often stay with his herds if a grazing area were some distance away. But then she heard the impatient sounds of sheep and goats. Why would he have left them penned till this hour?

She knew she shouldn't hover over Erlin, but she couldn't stop herself from leaving her task. She started toward the pen, her usual stout club in one hand, a cluster of grapes in the other. The grapes were ripe only about a month out of the year. She put one into her mouth and sucked on it awhile before finally biting down. The juice was pleasant, though sour, and each time she ate one she was tempted to spit out the tart skin. But she would swallow it instead, mindful of the long winter when she would long for the grapes.

Erlin was not near his flocks. At sight of Risha they began an indignant bleating that told her they had not been loosed that day.

Erlin was not in the fields with his father, either. Risha did not go and speak to Kael as she saw him laboring in mid-field, stooped like a great dark beetle under the sun. She walked to Erlin's favorite sites, apprehensive, yet reassuring herself there was some simple explanation. But none presented itself and she couldn't dismiss mental scenes of wild beasts attacking him. She was becoming alarmed enough to go to Kael, when she noticed the rocks marking the far edge of the field which Onar worked. Was it her imagination, or were they piled differently? The thing intrigued her and she walked across the field to the odd configuration.

Once there had been a small gully here. Now, large rocks filled the depression. She stepped up to them, frowning, and with her foot pushed one precariously balanced; it tumbled away. She bent over and pulled three of the large rocks off the pile, and as she removed the last one, the blood drained from her face. A portion of a human shoulder could be seen in the opened crevice.

She suddenly grabbed the rocks firmly in her hand and pitched them away. As she dislodged a long, flat one, she saw an ear and hair and knew immediately that it was Erlin. She quickly threw the other stones from his face, longing to believe it wasn't true, but his full features came into view, motionless and smeared with dirt.

She tore away more of the stones covering her son and cast them away. One after another she grasped and flung away, unmindful of the small cuts and abrasions on her hands. Erlin lay on his side, and as she removed each rock and saw more of his body, she steeled herself against the rage building in her, still hoping that somehow he might be saved, might still be coaxed into life. It took only moments to uncover him. Quickly she knelt close beside him and gently turned his face toward hers. It was unblemished, except for streaks of dirt. She wiped at them, and felt his mouth with her fingers and then touched his eyes, and kissed them. But she detected not the smallest response.

She raised herself a little on her elbow and moved his head. There, dried blood entangling disheveled hair, was the wound, broad and deep. Although she had never seen a man killed, she knew well the results of such a wound, and her faint hopes which she had been fight-

ing to keep alive died immediately. She let her elbow collapse into place beside her and with her other arm over her son's body, wept.

Who or what had done this? Who had covered her son with these unfeeling rocks? She tried to put out of her mind the image of Onar. It was always Erlin who had pleased Aaael, making his brother jealous. Hadn't Aaael warned Onar that sin desired to have him,

131

crouched and ready to devour him? But surely he wouldn't murder his brother! She thought of the evil forces she had confronted. They must have done this!

Erlin dead. The only thing in this accursed world she really cared about destroyed. All that Erlin was to give to her, to his sons—all his creativity, his laughter, the songs he would have sung, the love he would have given, all he was to be, gone. She could more easily endure the loss of the sun.

She rose, disheveled, and looked down at her ruined son. Risha steeled herself against the desire to weep beside him again, and instead forced herself to plan how she could bring him home. She knew he was too big for her to carry, but she could not—would not—leave him. If she could get her shoulder under his chest, she might have enough leverage.

She knelt beside him and lifted. His head dropped down lifelessly as she raised him, and the finality of that motion cut through her. But she continued lifting and succeeded in getting herself partially erect under him. Then she tried to move but found it exceedingly difficult. He seemed far heavier in death; if he were sleeping, she wondered, would he weigh her down like this? Anger came to her aid, for she couldn't stand leaving him here among those rocks. She heaved with all her strength, dragging Erlin's limp form across the field step by staggering step, digging one foot into the dirt, then giving a mighty shove forward for another foothold.

She pressed on, but her body started shaking with the effort when she was not more than halfway back. When she saw the hill before her, she knew she couldn't climb with Erlin on her. She eased her son down in the middle of the field, gently nestled his head on a clump of grass, and stayed on her knees beside him. Then she rose, her cheek and shoulders smeared with her son's blood, and walked quickly ahead.

As soon as she topped the hill, she saw across the meadow a man standing with Kael. Instantly, she knew who it was.

Aaael himself was conversing with Kael. She looked about for a retinue of great ones, for Shia or others, but Aaael stood alone. She stopped, shocked by a new question. What did this mean? Had evil outwitted Aaael? Was that possible? Surely he knew of Erlin's death —why else would he be here? Yet . . . if he knew, why hadn't he stopped this atrocity!

Surely he could not know, she thought. Then she remembered Erlin's blood upon her, and she blanched at the realization she could be accused. She felt fear only for an instant; it was replaced by anger. "Let it be so!" she said aloud. "That would tell me everything about Aaael," and she started walking resolutely toward the two figures in the distance. Before she came close to them, however, Aaael broke away from her husband and walked toward her. She continued to advance, trembling, her disheveled, begrimed state giving her a feeling of heroism, of a woman grievously wronged. But as soon as she was close enough to see Aaael's face fully, she realized he understood all and was full of compassion toward her. He said nothing as they met, but only reached out to her and grasped her hands firmly. She stood looking into his face, feeling the strength of his hands upon hers. They continued looking at each other, the horror of Erlin's death heavy in the air. No words were spoken, yet she knew he grieved with her. The moments passed and she was loath to release his hands or his gaze. But then she was aware, through Aaael's motion, that Onar was also in the camp, for Aaael had turned his head toward her elder son.

She watched as Aaael walked toward Onar, who stood by the mouth of the cave, erect, his face intense. Aaael stopped several paces from him and looked into his eyes as he had into Risha's. But she couldn't see Aaael's expression, only her son's, inscrutable except for a cheek muscle which twitched and betrayed him.

The words from Aaael not only broke the silence but shattered Risha's composure. "Where is your brother Erlin?"

Onar's face remained stiff as he responded in clipped, deliberate words, "How do I know? Am I my brother's keeper?"

Risha had moved beside Kael, and her son's answer chilled her, for she saw his struggle to make his face a mask. Finally her rage had an object. Onar, who had always hated Erlin, had finally murdered him. There he stood, trying to hide the monstrous change in the universe— Erlin never breathing and laughing and talking again, Erlin covered up like a battered animal. As she glared with growing fury at Onar, she heard Kael's anguished whispers beside her: "Onar. Onar. My son. Do not slay him, Aaael," he was pleading. "Do not slay him."

Slay him? Risha jerked her head toward Kael and their eyes met. *Would Aaael slay him?* The grisly possibility that Aaael would execute her son turned her thoughts. If she and Kael were banished into all this misery for a piece of fruit, what ought Onar to suffer for murder? Her fury against Onar was turning to alarm. She desired vengeance, yet would it satisfy her? The mental images, rising unbidden, of Aaael executing her son caused her to inwardly cry out against them.

Aaael spoke, his words reverberating like the crash of high waves against cliffs. "What have you done? Your brother's blood cries out to me from the ground. You have defiled the ground with your brother's blood, and you are therefore cursed of it. When you work, the ground will not yield crops. You'll be a fugitive, a wanderer." The words were stated with finality, with an infinite sadness.

Risha observed the muscles in Onar's jaws, and his eyes. The pronouncement had stunned him. Fugitive. The ground cursed. The only thing which had ever really responded to him, she realized—the ground—would now be his enemy. She heard Onar crying out, his voice shaking, that he could not bear such a punishment. "You have

134

banished me from my work and from you. Everyone who sees me will try to kill me!" Onar's eyes did not shift to those of his mother, but she sensed his fear of her vengeance.

"I will repay seven times your punishment on anyone who kills you," Aaael said, and with a simple motion put his mark upon Onar as a warning. He stood between the parents and son, looking intently at the young man. If Aaael communicated further to him, Risha was unaware of it. For long moments they all stood there, motionless, and then Aaael gestured Onar away. Onar looked at his mother and his father, but their expressions were impassive. He turned and walked woodenly up an incline. After a few paces, he picked up a stick, then disappeared over a hill. At the last glimpse of his back, Risha dropped her eyes to the ground.

Aaael stood nearby, silent. She found herself on her knees before him, weeping, and she could never be sure afterwards if she had heard his voice or just remembered it from so many years ago, but it moved clearly into her mind, Aaael's voice saying, "Be fruitful, and multiply, and replenish the earth." The command repeated itself again and again, gasping alone in her mind like a single fish sucking for air in a dying pond. She had no strength left to grapple with the idea. She kneeled, numb, trying to find some rock upon which to rest, trying to concentrate on Aaael's face and hands, but trying not to remember Aaael's final words to Onar.

When she looked up, Aaael was gone. No one but her husband was in the camp, and he stood like a tree stripped of its leaves and limbs, his face contorted, leaning against a wall of rocks. Risha found herself very slowly rising to her feet, then walking swiftly toward the empty horizon, suddenly convinced that more important than protecting the lifeless body of Erlin, more important than speaking to Kael, was her need to confront Onar, to catch him before he was beyond her reach.

AFTER crossing the meadow and the fields which Onar would no longer till, Risha ran in the direction she thought he would have gone, along the river and near the far woods. She followed the path of the trapline until it curved to the left, and then she moved quickly to a little hill from which she could survey the river, woods, and meadows. At first she saw nothing, but then a movement far off at the edge of the forest caught her eyes, and she knew immediately it was Onar. She ran down the gentle incline, racing through the tall grass, hoping to reach him before he moved into the woods. She darted out of the tall grass and into the leaves of the forest floor just in time to hear a rustling ahead. In a moment she was only a dozen paces from him, and he turned with a look of fear.

His grip tightened on his stick. Risha, seeing his hunted look, became aware of the stout club in her own hand and her grief-ravaged intensity. "I have not come to kill you," she said. "Seven times your punishment would be too much even for me to bear."

Risha was immediately saddened; she had not meant to sound caustic. "Why do you hunt me then?" Onar demanded.

She did not know herself, only that she had to confront him. This time she carefully planned her words. "How could I not come? Onar, you're my own flesh." Her grief for Erlin still kicked like a mortally wounded creature within her. Yet she felt she was guilty herself, and her grief for her living son—who was just as dead to her now as Erlin—caused Risha to cry out, "Onar, am I not destroyed when you murder both my sons? You have murdered yourself. Your blow against Erlin struck your own head; his blood has not only stained your hands but has soaked into your very bones."

136

Onar stood with not the slightest change of expression, as if expecting an attack of some sort. "Why tell me the obvious, Mother?"

"I'm not here to hurt you!" she protested. "My soul cries out to you that we are devastated *together,* and that I've helped bring this grief on you. Onar, you're my son!" She stopped talking, then forced the next words out like a violent act against herself. "Haven't I tempted you with harsh words, with my love for Erlin? Don't I share your guilt?"

Onar's expression slightly softened, and after a moment his body shifted to a position leaning against his stick. But his eyes continued to search his mother's face. "We are both stained," she said. "I was outraged when I saw Erlin dead. It devastates me. But I can't despise you as my rage insists. I am you.

"My son! What monstrous forces are about us, or in us?"

The young man ground his teeth, then slumped to a sitting position on the ground, hunching himself forward against the lengthening shadows of the forest. Risha wondered if her face looked as wasted as his. He continued to hunch over, staring, and Risha kept silence, afraid to say more, fearing she might chide him again.

She noticed then there were tears in Onar's eyes, and they began dripping down his face, but he remained motionless. His expression was not one of weeping. He sat staring, with the tears flowing from his eyes like fluids from the body of a punctured corpse. Finally he spoke. "Why have we been cursed, Mother? Left out in the fields to die?"

"You need not die, Onar—"

"A slow and hateful death," Onar interrupted. "Will I survive alone in the forest? Away from Aaael, left to the evil? And if I survive, will I want to? Why have I been singled out for this heinous thing? Was I made for this?"

"Do not ask!" Risha nearly shouted. "It's too terrible a question! You were warned. Aaael himself warned you that sin crouched at the

137

door, and you heard his warning—" Risha stopped short and blanched. She did not know if Onar read her thoughts of the warnings she had received in the garden. But he said nothing, although his eyes were keen with fear.

After an interminable pause, he asked her simply, "If Aaael loves us so much, if we are his children, how could he let all this happen?"

She could respond at first only with silence. At last she said, "Onar, that's what I ask myself every morning. I awake and realize I am banished and condemned."

"Aaael!" Onar suddenly shouted, bounding up from the ground, beginning to talk with animated gestures. "How can we know he is any different from the others? Good? Bad? Both? He comes with his warnings and lays them upon us, and we have years and years to make *one* mistake, and then we are crushed like a beetle between his fingers. In one burst of passion I have become accursed! We are to honor and love him, but didn't he make us as we are? Has he no responsibility?"

Risha breathed heavily. "You are your mother's son," she said, shaking her head. "But Onar, you murdered your brother. You planned it. You took him to the field. It was your hand, your will."

"And you ate the fruit! And Father, too. Have you forgotten? But it was inevitable, so why the self-hatred? Aaael could easily bring Erlin back to life again. But he has rules: our disobedience brings death. It's like a child's game—"

Risha felt weakened and confused by the vehemence of his frantic arguments; they seemed like fingers of a drowning creature upon a raft. A question stabbed into her thoughts, and she voiced it. "Who!" she demanded. "To whom have you been talking? Who has fed you these ideas?"

Onar took a sudden breath of air through his nostrils and glared at her. He was caught off guard, but he didn't hesitate to answer: "You know, Mother. It is ever the same."

138

So—the evil forms had seduced her son. She felt relief at being able to direct her wrath against them. They had been pawns, both of them.

But she knew this would not do. No matter how much she wanted to embrace the idea, this was the very thought the evil forces insinuated into their minds, the very arguments of the serpent and Uilades.

A noise which sounded like a small animal startled them, and then they heard a voice. Kael. Was he here? Of course, Risha thought, would he have let her come running after her son and not followed? Didn't he long for Onar even more than she—Kael, who had worked beside him, taught him the use of the hoe and blade? His voice was near, almost as if he were already part of their conversation. "We are made like Aaael himself," Kael insisted, emerging from the shadows of dusk. "We are not mere animals. We are of Aaael. Don't you believe there is evil in the world, Onar? That evil corrupts and cannot be called good? Onar, evil corrupted all of us to blaspheme Aaael." His words were strong, but his face showed a father's longing for his son. Kael reached toward him and drew his only living son to his embrace and wept upon his chest.

Onar at first was stiff and unyielding, merely tolerant. But then he slowly began to return his father's embrace. Risha felt outside whatever comfort they were finding in each other; she moved to them and put her arms around them, pulling them tightly against her breasts.

They stood together, and Risha thought she heard Onar softly weeping, and once she thought he whispered, "I am afraid. I am afraid." But the sounds were nearly inaudible and she wondered if she did not imagine them. It had become dark, but still they stood there, just inside the forest's edge, holding one another. When they finally moved apart, Kael put a bundle into Onar's hand and whispered something into his ear. Then he touched his wife's shoulder and led her back toward the camp, looking up to the stars and trees against the sky to find their way.

Onar is alone, she thought. *We were thrust out, but we had each other. Onar is utterly alone.* She grieved for both her sons, and whether one grief was greater than the other at that moment, she could not tell.

How could a bite of fruit change the world? But one quick motion of a club had devastated hers. Erlin's body lay waiting for them, gruesome testimony to the significance of one act.

CHAPTER FOURTEEN

KAEL hoisted his son upon his back and bent over, letting the feet drag behind him. Even in the dark, it had not been difficult to locate Erlin's body where Risha had left it. Now they stepped slowly, carefully under the starlight, three indistinct figures moving through the grasses. They reached the cave and started a fire, as much for cheer as for warmth. They did not place Erlin's body where he usually slept, near the entryway, but beside their own bed, to be near him.

The man and woman didn't speak but wearily made the fire, washed, and ate dried meat and corn. They lay down exhausted, with the body of their son between them. Risha wondered how it could be that the night before he had slept near them, fully alive, breathing softly, his flesh warm, but now lay between them lifeless. She couldn't draw close to him without soon feeling the chill from his body. At last she rose, patting Erlin on the shoulder, and moved around to Kael's side. Only his fingers were touching the body of Erlin, and when she moved beside him he pulled her close and drew the skins over them for warmth.

She awakened very late, nearly mid-morning, hearing the impatient bleating of the flocks. Risha knew she'd had a deep yet disturbing sleep, with many dreams, but she couldn't recall any of them. Her first awareness as she woke was of some lethal weight on her, pressing her against the dirt. *I'm like the snake under my boulder,* she thought, and then yesterday's events crowded into her mind like a wriggling mass of vipers. "Kael," she called. She looked about, then saw him standing at the entrance, the light on his face. *How long has he stood there?* she wondered.

"Kael," she called again, but he didn't respond. *What did he think,* she asked herself with some alarm, *of my words with Onar, of my confession to him? How does he judge my part in the murder?* Whatever his reactions, she would face the day; what did anything matter now that the thin strands of meaning she'd been holding on to during the past years had been severed? She stared at Kael for a very long time, watching his jaw muscles tighten, his face harden, then go flaccid.

Suddenly he cried out softly, "O, Aaael, put some truth into me! The woman's words pierce like arrows, and Onar's face shrivels my soul. How can we live in the world after *this*?" Risha listened to his moans, but she did not stir.

It was nearly noon before Kael stepped back into the cave and picked up some cakes to eat.

They sat at the entrance with the simple meal, the insistent bleating of the goats incongruous in the distance. "What will we do with Erlin?" Risha asked. She was looking at his face and saw the pain there and the fresh welling of moisture in his eyes. But he answered with only a little hesitation: "We must give him back to the ground."

Since she had discovered his body, she had felt some nameless dread about what would happen to Erlin now. Was a human like other flesh, mere meat and hair, subject to the desecration of worms or teeth? Or were they truly of Aaael like Shia?

"Couldn't Aaael take him?" she asked. "Placed on the altar, perhaps, he would draw him to the stars, to Shia's world. Or—"

"He must be returned to the earth. It's the will of Aaael," her husband said painfully. "He told me it must be so."

Looking into his face, she knew it was as grievous a moment for him as for her. She asked no more but ate silently, staring into the shadows where Erlin's body lay. Both dawdled over their meal. After Risha took a last drink from her cup, she turned to Kael. "Did you hear everything Onar and I said to each other?"

Her husband nodded. "I didn't want to disturb you."

"You've always been a better father than I a mother. I should have been slain with Erlin or banished with Onar."

"If you, then I also. Haven't I pushed all the guilt on you? Did I try to reconcile you and our children? I was too harsh with Onar!"

"You tried, once, to be reconciled with me, but I wouldn't let you."

"I did try. But trying once in all those years wasn't enough," he said in agitation. "Risha, I thought I could walk with Aaael, having given you and Onar warnings. But I never yearned for him—or for you. Aaael whispered to me, but I shut that off. I talked to him of other things, for I wanted to be righteous! I wanted to be righteous! So I added to your guilt. I walked with Aaael, but deep within I welcomed your resistance—"

"You're too hard on yourself," Risha said. "Onar's guilt and mine are our own."

"No! The closer I get to Aaael, the more clearly I see my damnable pride. I was angry with you and refused to be healed of my anger. But enough of our guilt. We've seen the depth of evil we've brought on our children, but we must begin afresh...."

Afresh! After all this, were they to attempt children again? Was it to go on and on like this, spending decades raising them, only to lose them to the powers of evil? How could she give birth to another child and nurse it and teach it and tell it of Aaael who loved them? "Be fruitful and multiply." The command mocked her.

Kael saw her distress and did not speak again. He walked to the body of his son and tenderly moved him onto a large skin. Then he lifted him under the arms and pulled him from the cave. Risha picked up the piles of soft foxtail barley that made up his bed, heaped them high on her arms so she could barely see over them, then followed. Kael dragged his burden toward the altar. He came to within twenty paces of it; there he stopped and laid Erlin's body tenderly beside a gully. Then he returned for a wooden spade he had fashioned years ago. He dug the gully to a greater depth as Risha stood beside her son's inert form, watching.

When he had completed his task, Kael motioned for Risha to place the bedding on the fresh earth, and slowly, with great reluctance, she did so. She stepped down, hating the touch of raw earth on her shoulders, and laid all of it carefully in place. After this, she climbed out and sat beside the grave. At Kael's gesture to pick up the body with him, she impatiently waved him away. She sat at the edge, staring at Erlin's body, remembering scene after scene with her boy, trying to seal them in her mind before they escaped. Only once did she speak aloud of them. "The thunderstorm. Do you remember the thunderstorm?"

Kael did not.

"When Erlin was only three, he was frightened by thunder," she said. "So every time a storm came, you and I and little Onar would say in happy anticipation, 'Oh, wonderful! Maybe we will hear the thunder!' We did this many times, clapping our hands and pointing to the lightning. And then remember the day of the big storm and the loudest thunder of all, and Erlin clapping and shouting at it instead of cowering in the corner, and Onar pointing to him in triumph? I can still see their faces side by side, with Erlin catching Onar's excitement." Risha paused. "You should remember. The idea to teach Erlin was yours."

Kael nodded. "I remember," he said.

Risha stared at her hands. How often since the expulsion had she wondered whether her hands would someday be dead flesh and bone. It seemed impossible. Now her son's hands—he who was younger and stronger—her son's hands were stiff.

144

She looked at her boy, refusing to have him lowered into the bedding she had prepared for him. Outraged goats bleated in the distance; mosquitoes lighted on her and bit her, but she took no notice. Then a bird, an orange thrush with a slight edge of blue on its wings, searching for insects in the field, landed at Erlin's foot. It skittered about and finally hopped up on the knee of the corpse. It triggered a strange reaction in her, this living thing on her dead son. She resented it, thought of calling out to it, chasing it away. But she didn't move nor call out; she merely watched the bird, its eye investigating, its feet moving saucily on Erlin's leg.

The bird flew off when Kael shifted his weight, and Risha at last rose and addressed herself to the task. She and Kael slid Erlin to the edge, then lowered him in the skin to the bedding below. Looking down, she saw he was half covered by shadows and she turned away quickly to gather flowers to place on his body. Three times she did this, carefully dropping them on him, forcing herself to let them float down on his face, trying to memorize it even as they fell. At last he was completely covered. Then they waited silently a very long time before Kael rose to cover him.

"No!" Risha objected, "one thing more," and her voice cutting the morning's long silence sounded out of place. She walked swiftly back and entered the far end of the cave, kneeling where Erlin had so often played and worked. She picked up several smooth, black stones with gold flecks he had played with as a little boy; a stone hammer he had used to crack nuts, and an oblong piece of bark he had worn on his clothing years ago. She tried to keep her eyes from similar playthings in Onar's corner. At the grave site, she lay on her stomach and reached down to her son under the grasses and flowers and carefully placed the items on him. As she stretched halfway down, she felt a longing to lower herself the rest of the way, to join Erlin. *If Kael were not here,* she thought to herself, *I would surely throw myself on my son and pray for the earth to swallow us together.*

145

But she rose from her extended position and stood awkwardly with her hands empty. When Kael began pushing the soft earth in upon the grave and she heard it hit, she turned suddenly and walked away.

Kael found her sitting in the river meadow with the goats and the sheep who were finally drinking and feeding. He sat beside her and reached out to touch her hand. She responded to his gentle pressure by intertwining their fingers. "What have we now but each other?" she asked.

"We have that. But we haven't lost Erlin forever. I swear it." Her fingers involuntarily slipped from his and she looked at him. He spoke again. "It's not Erlin under the earth; it's only the body he used. He's with Aaael, as Shia is. As we will be."

"How do you know?" she asked.

"Aaael keeps whispering it into my soul."

She waited, but he did not expand on his statement. "How monstrous!" she said suddenly. "Can't we at least see him once? Must we hold on to misty hopes and whisperings? Let me *know* Erlin races among the stars with Shia and I am content! But how terrible to hint at it! Ah, we must take it all by faith. Faith in *what!* Look at us *now!* We are to go on and bring forth more sons?" She buried her face in her hands.

After a time, Kael pulled her to her feet and walked with her among the flocks. Eventually she said to him, "I have always hated your altar. But I have always feared you were right and that I deserved all my torment! I've been at war with you, and at war with Aaael. I've wanted his power and glory, but not his telling me what to do! I'm like a tree cut off from the ground. There's nothing but decay in me, my desires, my imagination, my hatreds. I despise all the filth within, but I can't change it! I can't change *me*!"

They had stopped at the river's edge and Risha was facing the water, her back to Kael. He put his hands on her shoulders, but did not turn her around as he said, "We have the altar."

"I'll burn myself upon it," she said. "I'll burn quickly, like old, dry wood!"

"You may," said Kael. "But the fire which must consume us is Aaael's holiness."

"Yes, the flames of the altar purify. But Onar is banished from it."

"Perhaps! But Risha, why do you always object? Why do you talk of Aaael's grace as if it were capricious?"

"Why indeed?" she moaned.

CHAPTER FIFTEEN

THREE years had passed since the death of Erlin and the banishment of Onar. For three years Risha and Kael had labored alone, fought sickness, shivered through winter, and sweated through summer. They spoke only when necessary, and never sang. Loneliness and a sense of deepening tragedy pressed them together; they wondered if one died what would happen to the other. Death was always close. Yet they would look to the altar and its promise and labor on.

In the spring, for six days Risha couldn't eat breakfast; on the seventh she said to Kael, "I must go to the altar." Until then, she had never offered a sacrifice but had only participated in Kael's offerings.

"You've been upset for days; even your hands are trembling," Kael said kindly. Risha looked down at her right hand and pressed it firmly against her leg. "I wish I could be happy about the seed in me and enjoy watching your face brighten as I tell you. But there's no joy, only turmoil."

Kael took this announcement of his impending fatherhood with a broad smile, obviously considering it good news whatever Risha felt at the moment. He took her hand. "Risha, what does the altar have to do with this? It's a time to rejoice!"

She left her hand in his but turned her face away. "Kael, Onar keeps appearing in my mind. I'm afraid I'll hold my baby and think of holding him, or Erlin. I'll watch my child play and wonder when the hatred will start. And how will I tell my child about his brothers? The baby grows, but I can't remove the curse!"

Kael listened, and when she had finished speaking, he said, "I'll make the preparations for the altar."

"The stones," she said. "But I must do the rest."

Kael looked at her sharply. She did not know if he disliked her taking his prerogatives or was concerned about the difficulty of the task. But he didn't object. He simply said, "I'll do my part now. Before dusk, I'll wait for you."

Now that Risha had committed herself, her hands began to tremble more visibly. She would meet Aaael this day. Would he see through her outward motions at the altar to her bitterness and reject her? She felt impure, unable to please him. *I've been rejected before,* she thought, *but now, perhaps, I'll be rejected in front of Kael and perhaps more devastatingly.* Yet she proceeded with her plan, for her only hope was at the altar.

In the afternoon she selected a young lamb, for it was always these downy, soft creatures she loved most. She sharpened the black-stoned blade and made all the preparations. Then she led the little lamb, which bleated occasionally, to the altar. She found it frightening to be clutching the soft wool in her own hands as Kael stood watching a short distance away. Yet she thrust in the blade and bled the lamb from the throat, then proceded to lay it whole upon the altar. *Like me,* she thought, *all of me, ready to be consumed by Aaael's wrath.*

Risha knelt before the altar, not wanting to light the kindling under the dead lamb. Only once had fire come out of heaven to consume the sacrifice, and that had been a sign to Kael. She wanted it to happen again, for she was coming to Aaael as he had, fully desiring him. *Or am I?* she wondered. *How can I see myself? I don't want you, Aaael, I admit it, since you know my every thought anyway. I've never wanted you enough to obey.*

Aaael, I'm corrupt! Now the seed is in me, and I start again. Aaael, I know now I'm not homesick for the garden nor even for Erlin, but for you. All the freedom I reached for has chained me. I'm trussed up, bound by my urges, bound by my homesickness, by my double-mindedness. I've been a rebel since the first taste of the fruit! Yes, Shia was right! What a bitter irony that I should reach for freedom only to receive this. *How could I shed* you, *Father?*

No celestial flame had touched the altar, though she knelt before it, fervently confessing her sins. She reached for the burning wick she had placed on the ground and lighted the dry twigs. The fire caught quickly and its heat drove her back several paces. She knelt again and called out to Aaael to receive her offering. *Only you can make me alive,* she called. *I can't quicken myself!* As the flaming wood became glowing coals and the odors of burning flesh and wool assailed her, she humbled herself before the creator and longed for release from her chaos. "Aaael!" she shouted, "I refused to commune with your voice! You have always been near me, but I've always pushed you away. I've longed for my own self, I've chased my own lies."

She spoke in great agitation for hours, and when she was least thinking of any purpose behind her supplications, something did begin happening within her. Like fire at the edge of a field, Aaael's peace invaded a small corner of her soul and then spread wider and wider until finally she began to feel contrite, and tears started flowing. She began to sense such release that she looked at the altar, half expecting flames to be shooting to the sky with this power building in her. But they were not. She didn't care. All she knew was that everything was different now, that her relationship with Aaael was changed, and that her weeping was more joyful than any laughter of the past years. She wept and communed with Aaael till the tears dried on her cheeks and then she rose before the now smoking altar and sang out in praise to the night sky.

As she sang with a loud voice, Shia stood in the smoke and moved forward to her, reaching out with her hands. Risha ceased singing, but Shia joined in the praise and bade her sing with her. The two voices sounded through the fallen world.

Then Risha knelt before Shia and pleaded, "Tell me all, and this time I will listen. Tell me of life and of Aaael and I will not stop you with questions." Shia would not let her kneel but helped her rise, and the two of them walked through the fields and the forest in the night, their way illumined by Shia's radiance. They rejoiced in the purity of Aaael as Shia revealed much to Risha, who was filled with gratitude. "And I had hoped for an ascending flame," Risha declared as Shia led her back to the camp, "but I received both Aaael and you! I could want nothing more!"

"But you shall have more," Shia said. "By your seed, things will happen that I couldn't even imagine. By your seed will come the wonder and joy of the universe." Shia lifted the woman in her luminous arms and carried her to her bed, for Risha was exhausted from her night of contrition and exaltation. "This is the night of your cleansing. You must always remember it, for such signs will never come to you again in the world. The next time you see me, most beloved Risha, you'll be with Erlin and with Aaael." And before Risha could think or move or protest, Shia was gone and the night was dark once more.

KAEL'S head and broad back descended a few feet below Risha as they followed a trail to the forest's floor in search of nuts. She carried an empty goatskin bag over her shoulder and wondered about the difficulty of climbing back later. Halfway down, her foot slipped on rotted leaves and wet moss covering a rock and she jerked her

152

weight to the side to regain her balance. She then found herself running down the incline, gathering momentum, despite her efforts to grab a branch to break her speed. She was alarmed for the eight-month fetus within her.

At her first scream, Kael had spun around and was already scrambling toward her. Suddenly she went sprawling down hard among the rocks and trees, just missing Kael's rushing, protective hands.

"Are you all right? I almost got to you!" Kael exclaimed, reaching down to her. "An instant. Just an instant and I would have caught you."

"And crashed with me," she said. She rolled onto her back and touched her distended belly, rubbing her palm gently over it. "No matter," she said lightly. "I don't think the fall hurt the baby." But she realized, after her initial relief, that her face and arm were badly scraped and bruised, and that her knee was swelling.

Kael began to inspect the abrasions.

"Nasty," he said. "I'll carry you home and we'll soak them."

"We're here to gather nuts, at the *bottom* of the hill. Why go up and then come back? The squirrels will have them all by then." Kael tried to persuade her, but she insisted they continue their task. "At least I'll carry you to the trees," he said, and lifted her into his arms and carefully picked his way along the path. She didn't resist but put her cheek against his and gripped his neck lightly, ignoring the stings of the scrape on her wrist. They came to the first of the hickory trees and he settled her down comfortably with her back against it. "I'll help you gather," she said, insistent.

"You will not," he insisted with more vehemence than she, and peeled, then cracked a nut for her between his strong fingers.

She smiled as she settled against the trunk. "Thank you," she said. "In this, I don't mind your being stronger. In fact, you may have noticed that recently I haven't minded your strength in many things."

As Kael climbed a tree and began picking above her, she thought about their new responsiveness to each other since the seed was in her. Part of it, she thought, is that he doesn't have the preeminence in everything. He can't nurse the baby. He can't feel an elbow or foot move under his skin. I'm experiencing the new life, but Kael can only watch.

Kael found her in this contented mood when he sat beside her to shell, one bag full from the tree above. They worked together, at times having to beat half-ripe skins against the stones to dislodge them. "Kael," she asked, "how can we be so loving to each other at one moment, and bitter and carping the next?"

He brushed a pile of shells from his lap. "Because we don't listen to Aaael's voice within us."

"But we have! Both of us have been filled with his fire and power and have thrown ourselves into his cause. At those moments we transcend our pettiness. But hours later we find ourselves haggling over a cracked water jug. How can we be such changeable creatures?"

Kael continued shelling. Risha was glad he didn't reply superficially, as he often did. He had shelled at least a dozen more nuts before he sighed deeply and said, "We're just not the same as we were in the garden. And twenty years of carping aren't purged in one night of Aaael's presence."

"Why not?" she asked.

"Questions. Always you have questions," he said, his eyes twinkling. "I thought you were done with questions and would listen from now on."

"Yes," she said quietly. "But sometimes a question is necessary for me to listen. Didn't Aaael himself put my curiosity into me? Questions just spring into my mind. They can't all be from the evil ones."

Kael kept silent. She was tempted to say more, but patiently waited for him. "No," he finally said, "it's not possible all your questions

154

are evil. But you know when they're whisperings of the evil ones and the line is very thin between them. The enemy is subtle. He'll use what we are to destroy us, if he can."

"But why aren't we told more? All this subtlety? Why are we not clearly—"

"Shia told you many, many things. Aaael has revealed much. You know enough to obey and resist the evil . . ."

Risha noticed a squirrel climbing down a sapling toward Kael's pile of shelled nuts; its stealthy movements amused her and she smiled broadly. She looked up at Kael. "Here we are in the forest, together, and again we are too serious, discussing evil. Let's sing instead of the trees and the birds and the life within me!" They sang then, both of them, and Kael carried her home tenderly, the skins full of nuts hanging by his sides.

RISHA had anxiously awaited the birth, but week after week the baby had simply grown larger. When the pains had begun, the fetus was ten months and very large. She had been greatly relieved that it was finally to begin, and she had felt a thrill of anticipation despite the pain.

But that had been more than a day before. The pains had intensified. Now Risha lay upon layers of skins exhausted and frightened. The fire flickered against the cave walls as she pushed desperately.

She thought about animals she had seen in birth. None seemed to experience such pain. She had suffered intensely with Onar and Erlin, yet their births had been relatively quick. This one continued at the peak of her pains and she couldn't push him out.

Now! she screamed within herself as she pushed with all her strength, feeling just at the edge of victory. But still, no movement. She collapsed against the skins and thought of a sheep she had seen die because it could not give birth. Kael had finally slit its belly, and even then, the lamb had died also.

A chill touched her. Kael certainly *did* know what to do for animals. What was he thinking right now? She had been trying for hours to give birth. Was it too large to pass? Would she grow weaker and weaker? Would he have to make the choice of ripping the baby from her womb? Who would live? Risha? The baby? Neither?

Kael saw she was increasingly distraught and wiped her face again. "The next time the pains come, push—push with all your strength and pray to Aaael for more!"

She felt a trace of anger at his advice which she had already been following for so long. But this time his hands were on her shoulders; she girded herself and with a sharp cry used all the strength of her body.

But the baby would not move.

She felt frenzied. What more could she do? Why must her life continue from agony to death to anguish to more death? Surely Aaael wouldn't give her this seed of promise and not let her see it. Would he have her hold it in her arms as she died with her belly ripped open?

The pains returned, and she breathed deeply, and did all Kael instructed, grimacing with an effort that was beyond her physical powers.

And the child of promise was born.

CHAPTER SIXTEEN

THE old woman's eyes came back into focus and settled on the girl seated on the dirt floor across the room. The ancient Risha felt the spittle on her chin and focused her eyes on her blue-veined, thin hand, willing the flaccid flesh and bones to move. She wanted to be quicker than the younger woman and succeed in wiping her chin before she could cross the room. *But what does it matter?* Risha thought. *Trinidel has wiped my chin many times while my soul sought Aaael.*

"Mother," the young woman said apprehensively.

Mother, Risha thought. Every woman Risha had ever known or met through ten centuries had called her Mother. And every man—except Kael. *How is it possible,* Risha wondered, shaking with the effort of lowering her hand, *that I once lived in supple young flesh like this woman's!*

Risha had recovered traces of her *empath* sense, and she felt the fear in the young woman. "Trinidel, why are you so afraid?" she asked, longing to infuse her own peace into her daughter of so many generations.

"Mother, if only you stood strong and fierce, the way you did when your righteous anger led us against the pagans. Then we could rise up against them again," Trinidel said, distraught but reverential. "You could rouse us all in the holy cause."

"Trinidel," Risha said with effort, "it has taken me a thousand years to learn that desiring what cannot be brings only bitterness. Ask,

'What *is* Aaael doing, and how can I please him in it?' "

"Doing!" The young woman's shock at Risha's words overcame for an instant her awe of her Mother. "We are all about to be murdered. The name of Aaael will be thrown into the dung heap and all that's holy will be desecrated. My children's generations will never know him . . . my children won't even be born!"

Risha's weakened body slouched back in the rough leather-and-wood chair, Trinidel's emotions mixing with her own. The ancient Mother closed her eyes and rested a full moment, then opened them again slowly. "You don't know, Trinidel, the exceeding greatness of Aaael. He spins off a trillion suns at a breath; his mighty hosts extol him in strange and numberless worlds. He penetrates all, including this moment. He controls the enemy outside our gates. What does it matter if a tiny edge of his universe forgets a name we use for him?"

"Ancient Mother!" the woman exclaimed in great agitation, falling at her knees and weeping. "It's hard for me! You've seen Aaael, you know all, but I can't see past the destruction of my mother and my father and all I've ever known."

Painfully Risha stretched out her brown-spotted hands and touched the woman's hair. "Aaael has things planned for this planet far beyond our imaginations. He has drunk the cup for us. He is the promise. You've known and loved Aaael," she gently remonstrated.

Trinidel continued to weep and eventually whispered, almost inaudibly, "Yes. But not as you have."

"No. He has been a familiar terror to me. But his terror burns away the fear."

The ancient Mother stopped speaking and tried to give her peace to her daughter. But she sensed it would not work, for no others had the *empath* gift. She began talking to Aaael about Trinidel, about her fears and her future. She realized Trinidel wondered if she were senile, perhaps even wondered if she were not, after all, the mother of all but only an old crone with stories to tell. Yet she knew Trinidel wanted to believe and saw in the girl her own questioning youth. Risha was drained of the need for questions, had lived a millennium of questions. She was now already halfway into Aaael's other worlds.

Risha didn't realize as she communed with Aaael how much time had elapsed. When she reopened her eyes, Trinidel was seated again across the room. Trinidel, as soon as she noticed Risha was awake again, said, "They are above us on the hill, like marching ants. The sun glints from their swords and their shouts chill my very bones. . . ."

"Graethe has told you this?"

"Ancient Mother, I can *hear* them! But yes, he has told me. They can take us in moments."

"We can't live without grief and suffering," Risha said. "It's our story and part of our hope."

"But not to be destroyed!"

"You *cannot* be destroyed. You, Trinidel, will live longer than the stars. You are more permanent than the rocks or waters. Aaael has made nothing so eternal as a living soul. You will breathe and laugh and sing when our planet shudders in its death throes."

"I want to believe you, Mother, but the fear—"

"Believe Aaael!" she said. "I have lived a thousand years of fear and wounds and deepest pain. Suffering is fertile ground. From it we see the universe as it is. From it we see Aaael's redemption."

Trinidel's eyes again moved apprehensively toward the city gates.

"Help me to rise," the old woman commanded. She noticed Trinidel's momentary expression of hope which quickly faded. *She thinks me senile,* Risha thought, *but hopes against hope that I may yet deliver her by warfare.* "Put your arms under mine," Risha instructed. "We will go to the grave of Kael."

"Oh, no, Mother! It's near the gate. We'll be slain by the first invaders. You can't walk across the room, let alone through the city!"

The young woman tried to ease her charge back into the chair. But Risha's resolve was firm and she forced her body to rise.

"We are no more safe here than there. Trinidel, you will aid me," the ancient Mother commanded. The younger woman hesitated, but Risha's old legs, disfigured by red-and-purple veins like blotched spider webs, were moving resolutely toward the door. *I am a dessicated crone,* Risha said to herself with satisfaction and even an edge of humor. She thought it paradoxical that now in constant pain and blurred vision, with the world a mass of indistinct impressions, she should be more intently savoring life than she ever had since the expulsion.

But with every step they took in the city, Risha felt others' fear and heard the panicked scurrying. She watched through her rheumy eyes some children racing away from the view at the wall and felt their terror. She spoke to Aaael about them as she painfully advanced. She believed all the agonies of her city, and all the warring armies, had been caused by her own disobedience a millennium ago—but she no longer felt the guilt which for so long had eaten at her spirit. Instead, she felt gratitude for Aaael's forgiveness. Aaael kept whispering it to her, and she reached into the reservoirs of her centuries of communing with him to force her withered body forward and to overcome the trembling of the city, which continued pressing in upon her soul.

Trinidel silently assisted the frail, thin form advancing with such excruciating slowness. Finally they stood at the rocks where Risha had buried Kael more than a hundred years before. She stood, her shadow falling upon the stones, thinking of her centuries with this man.

"Trinidel, can you imagine what Kael and I shared all those generations?" Risha said aloud. "How many times did he lead our sons in battle? How many times did he turn thousands of our children to love

Aaael? You've heard much of his last battle, and his shouts, but only I saw his face as the arrow struck him, and his smile at its significance. He died urging us on, and in our rage at their killing Kael we routed those who came up against us. My grief was great, but tempered by that look as he died, as if he were amazed to be finally free."

She looked at the gray stones at her feet. "It's good to fight with the power of Aaael," Risha said, less to Trinidel than to the wind. "Yet it's an awesome danger to have Aaael's intensity. One can replace it with one's own intensity—or that of the serpent—and presumptuously spill blood in Aaael's name. Always err on the side of gentleness."

Her spirit surveyed the centuries and seemed to flow up and out of her shriveled body. She stood in two worlds. She felt she was with Kael on the city's walls, reaching up for the comet streaks of light before them, aware of thousands of Aaael's children beckoning . . . she continued to talk with Kael even as her body fell between the arms of Trinidel to the ground.

She revived in only a few moments, perhaps because of Trinidel's extreme discomfort, for she was rubbing Risha's face and exclaiming that it was madness to have come here and that she had erred in her duty. With the young woman's assistance, Risha brought her old remnant of a body to its feet again. A few yards away stones marked the place where, only a few years ago, she had buried her third son, Pela, the child of promise. Erlin's grave was beside it. Nearly a thousand years separated the deaths of her second and third sons. She wondered how they would appear when she saw them again. Risha felt an intense longing for Erlin, without the least doubt he was as alive as she, in fact, perhaps more so. She was trapped in this decrepit body, but was as alive and full of humor and joy as Erlin, wherever he was. So many sons and daughters dead, so many burials past, so many reunions soon upon her. She had no doubt she would walk with them.

Would Pela be old and Erlin young, though Erlin was actually older? What would she herself be like?

A horrendous shout from beyond the walls, like the screaming of grey hyenas, made Trinidel wince and turn toward the older woman. Risha touched her hand to the girl's cheek. "Child. They are only my sons, trying to frighten you."

"Sons? They humiliate! They smash our children's heads against the rocks, then laugh! They rip open the pregnant with the sword, then sing! They *worship* their swords in solemn rituals! They ravish the women and then spear them for sport!" Trinidel's dread reverberated into Risha's emotions and she shuddered with her.

"It is only death," she told her daughter. "The pain is great, perhaps, but short. Trinidel . . ." but her voice trailed off, for Risha didn't have the strength to talk over the shouting and she turned to retrace her steps. They had not gone fifty paces when Graethe ran up to them.

"Mother!" he exclaimed. Risha heard Graethe's remonstrances at her leaving her room, but she soon relapsed into the other world as he picked her up to carry her back.

When she became aware of her surroundings again, she was back in her room with Graethe standing before her, gesticulating at the door. "We will take you to the mountains," he was saying. "There's a chance. I must fight here, but three young men and three young women might be able to slip through to the river and—"

Risha attempted a smile, but her trembling old lips barely moved. "Why should I, of all in the city, be the one to escape?" she asked.

"Ancient Mother, you are all we have of power. You are the center. You're the hope of the people."

"Not me," she corrected. "Aaael. Send others to escape."

"We have. But Mother, we're a dying cult! Don't you understand? We can't withstand the enemy. Nothing rallies the people, and we're too few."

"Then give up. Serve them; but keep Aaael in your hearts."

"If we prostrated ourselves before them and begged for their peace, the barbarians would burn out our left eyes so we could never again fight with the sword. And they would make each man of us a eunuch!" He spoke with revulsion, and Risha slowly raised her eyes to meet his. "Die then," she told him. "Die with your sword in hand, and come dance with me, son, in the next world."

He leaned back heavily against the wall and grimaced. "All my life you have said such things." He paused. "I will die with my sword, Mother. But if the hordes which hate us annihilate you and Trinidel and everything drawing breath in this city, the light is gone everywhere."

Risha motioned for him to come closer. She stared with her diffused vision into his eyes and asked, "Son, do you believe in Aaael? Commune with him? Obey him?"

He hesitated, his eyes locked by hers. Finally he nodded assent to her questions. "Then rejoice that you and I and all our people in this city shall dance with him this day!" She made her declaration in a cracked but fervent voice. "For out of the maddening butcheries will come joy, and out of the murders shall come joy, and out of the wail of the horrified child shall come joy. For Aaael himself has drunk the cup. For Aaael himself shall drink the cup, Aaael himself is drinking the cup, yes, Aaael *himself.* Joy!"

Risha's conviction and power, conveyed in her tremulous voice, brought color to Graethe's large-boned face. They were words he had heard in rituals many times before, but in this context they nourished his spirit. He turned and pulled back a skin which hung between them and the city. Risha knew he wanted to believe and embrace her words, yet longed for her to rise and lead them in battle as she had with Kael and after Kael's death.

"How can we, the good, the righteous, the innocent, be des-

163

troyed?" he said. "How can we let evil obliterate all that is holy, all that *is*."

Her voice, interrupting, was almost indiscernible against his, but he stopped and listened in deference to her. "Aaael—not we—allows destruction, and allows edification. Joyous be Aaael's name."

Graethe countered passionately, looking out at the gray horizon, "The evil ones always destroy the good. Didn't it destroy you and Kael, our father? They devour the truth. They're only half human, perhaps not human at all, offspring of lost ones of Aaael mixing with the daughters of men. They're ravenous giants; their teeth are their swords come to hack our flesh. These blasphemous sons of Aaael ravish your daughters, and we all—all of us—are helpless!"

Risha watched the faces of her son Graethe standing and her daughter Trinidel sitting in the corner, receiving their emotions into herself, but unable to share with them her peace and power. She spoke with longing for them, "Aaael will preserve what he wishes to preserve. You think the evil shall win? *Never!*" she declared, and her voice on that word rose almost as loudly as Graethe's. "The evil shall be utterly destroyed! All of it! All of it! Even in its most barbarous power, it shall be blasted, and Aaael shall prevail!"

The screams of the conquerers became louder as they assaulted the gate. Trinidel rose trembling to her feet. "I believe, Mother. The shouts from the merciless outside are weaker than your little voice. But it's hard when I feel the fear." Risha felt Trinidel's and Graethe's fears penetrating her body as she communed with Aaael about all the sons and daughters she loved throughout the city. The old woman had difficulty maintaining her awareness, for she kept slipping off into other realities.

Raucous sounds, splintering wood, and the smell of fire assaulted Risha's senses and brought her back. Her eyes barely focused in time to see Graethe lunge with his sword against three men coming at him.

There were no heroics in his death. Graethe crumpled, blood welling out and staining his shirt from ugly slashes. *Graethe is there now,* she thought with satisfaction. *Would that Trinidel follows quickly!* But the young woman was being yanked from the room despite her furious kickings and thrusts with a dagger which they quickly tore from her hand. She felt compassion for Trinidel and for her thousands of sons and daughters being humiliated. She called on Aaael for strength to face the next moments. She called not for courage, because courage had grown in her for centuries. But she had little strength, and she knew she would need much.

Risha sat in the chair, refreshing herself in Aaael's presence, drawing from him the power. She sat with eyes closed when some commotion before her drew her back to this world. A very large man stood towering above her, and when she was able to focus her eyes, she saw the contemptuous look on his face. He loomed like a tree above her, more than a head taller than Graethe. "Wipe the drool from her," he commanded, and a man bent to use the cloth on her chin.

"Thank you, my son," she said in her frail voice. Her face was a resolute, seamed rock.

"Son?" the huge man retorted angrily. "Old woman, I have a mother, and a mother's mother. Your name is a stench. Your lies will be ground to fine dust and buried with you in your cowardly city."

"You are my own flesh—"

"I am king over all Tenelent," he interrupted.

"Who made you a king over your brothers—you who are my own flesh?" Risha asked angrily.

The massive man grasped his sword and pulled it menacingly from its scabbard. "You are not my flesh nor my mother."

With great effort, Risha raised herself to stand before him and looked up at his sturdy frame. The ancient face taunted with a slight smile. "No, perhaps you are not," she admitted, clearly but softly.

DEVELASCO ©80

She leaned far back so she could see his face. "I've heard you're clever with a knife. Are the eunuchs you make as fertile as you?"

The bellow of rage which broke from him gave Risha enormous satisfaction. She had guessed right. *For all his strength, he's as sterile as a donkey!* she thought. *For all his power, he and his evil brothers will die childless; they will never mongrelize my sons and daughters.* "If I am no mother of yours," she added, "then these men with you are not your brothers. Is that why they call you the bastard?"

Her deliberate provocation tightened his grip on the sword and he jerked it above his head. She sank back into her chair, her strength spent. As she felt the firmness of the chair beneath her, she forced out with great effort, "Do you send me home to all I love? Strike then!"

She felt, even before the words left her mouth, that she was rising up out of her chair with new power, with new young flesh expanding from her bones, shoving aside the flaccid skin and the thin crackling hair like an old, loose garment being dropped at her feet. She felt herself running in joy to a ledge above a vast sea where Kael was laughing with Erlin, and then they were all being led by the living stones and by Shia up and up and through, hearing Aaael's whispers, moving with the grace and spirit of young colts among the celestial glories. . . . Her heart was lifted, and her inner vision clear, but her eyes were ancient and rheumy as they looked up for that fraction of an instant at the blade which then split her skull and left her old, worn body in a discarded heap upon the chair.

Colophon

This book was designed by Tyndale House Publishers'
art director, Tim Botts. The text type is Bembo and was
composed on a Mergenthaler VIP by Nora M. Holmes,
Westmont, Illinois. The calligraphy is the work of Tim
Botts. The offset lithography and case binding were
done by R. R. Donnelley & Sons, Crawfordsville,
Indiana. The text paper is fifty-five-pound Sebago,
bulking 350 pages per inch. The endpapers are Willow
Green Multicolor Antique by Process Materials Corpo-
ration and the cover material is Joanna Western's
Kennett. The front cover and spine stamping dies were
engraved by William Ziegenhorn and Jerry McDivett,
Chicago. Color separations for the dust jacket were
made by Magna Graphic, Inc., Lexington, Kentucky.
The jacket was printed on eighty-pound Howard Text
Vellum by R. R. Donnelley & Sons.